"Dance with me, Nico," Caitlin whispered huskily, her body burning for his touch.

A current of heat ran through him and told him everything he needed to know about why he had been so careful until now to avoid holding her in his arms. Instinctively he knew how it would be to have her against him. She was satin, sweet-smelling skin, and soft curves. Everything lovely and desirable. And inside he was dying with need for her.

Caitlin stared up at him, her head back, the long line of her throat exposed, her hair streaming down her back. He put his arms around her and pulled her closer. Clouds of music and moonlight, drifts of sea breezes, and, most of all, Caitlin threatened his common sense. He was playing with fire, but he'd never had a burn that didn't heal. Where was the harm?

Caitlin was distantly aware that they weren't dancing. Not that she had really wanted to dance. If she'd had a conscious thought at all, it was that she wanted to learn the feel of his hard lines, strong arms, firm lips. *Him.*

"Nico," she said.

Slowly he wrapped long, silky strands of her hair around his hand until he controlled the position of her head. "Yes," he said "Yes." Then his mouth captured hers, and she was his. . . .

WHAT ARE *LOVESWEPT* ROMANCES?

They are stories of true romance and touching emotion. We believe those two very important ingredients are constants in our highly sensual and very believable stories in the *LOVESWEPT* line. Our goal is to give you, the reader, stories of consistently high quality that may sometimes make you laugh, sometimes make you cry, but are always fresh and creative and contain many delightful surprises within their pages.

Most romance fans read an enormous number of books. Those they truly love, they keep. Others may be traded with friends and soon forgotten. We hope that each *LOVESWEPT* romance will be a treasure—a "keeper." We will always try to publish

LOVE STORIES YOU'LL NEVER FORGET
BY AUTHORS YOU'LL ALWAYS REMEMBER

The Editors

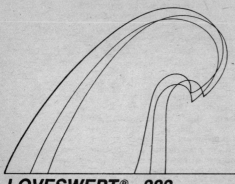

LOVESWEPT® • 383

Fayrene Preston
SwanSea Place:
The Legacy

 BANTAM BOOKS
NEW YORK • TORONTO • LONDON • SYDNEY • AUCKLAND

THE LEGACY

A Bantam Book / February 1990

LOVESWEPT® and the wave device are registered trademarks of Bantam Books, a division of Bantam Doubleday Dell Publishing Group, Inc. Registered in U.S. Patent and Trademark Office and elsewhere.

If you would be interested in receiving protective vinyl covers for your Loveswept books, please write to this address for information:

Loveswept
Bantam Books
P.O. Box 985
Hicksville, NY 11802

ISBN 0-553-22035-7

Published simultaneously in the United States and Canada

Bantam Books are published by Bantam Books, a division of Bantam Doubleday Dell Publishing Group, Inc. Its trademark, consisting of the words "Bantam Books" and the portrayal of a rooster, is Registered in U.S. Patent and Trademark Office and in other countries. Marca Registrada. Bantam Books, 666 Fifth Avenue, New York, New York 10103.

PRINTED IN THE UNITED STATES OF AMERICA

O   0 9 8 7 6 5 4 3 2 1

Preface *1894*

He stood with his back to the ocean, his gaze on the great house before him. *SwanSea.* Edward Trahern smiled. The house was truly a monument . . . a monument to him.

He had heard that next year in New York City, Mrs. Cornelius Vanderbilt would open her five-million-dollar house on Fifth Avenue. And it was said that Mrs. William C. Whitney was also planning a grand residence on Fifth Avenue. But he had commissioned the great Chicago architect, Louis Henry Sullivan, had worked closely with him, and he was satisfied that when people spoke in superlatives about a house, they would speak of SwanSea. Here on this wild, beautiful, windswept shore of Maine, the house would stand forever, a symbol of his life's accomplishments.

The morning sun rose behind Edward, spreading its golden warmth over the house. Like a giant fan-shaped seashell, the house symbolized the ocean that he had crossed to reach America. The back was narrow, softly rounded, and faced the sea. From there it fanned outward, northwest and southwest, in a series of horizontal structures that mirrored the waves behind him and offered an unobstructed view of the sea from the majority of the rooms. The front was a broad, curving expanse with a long, graceful skirt of white steps. Elegant curvilinear iron-work formed the balcony railings, and friezes of flowers and twisting, trailing vines decorated the facade.

Its four main stories represented the four decades of his life thus far; the next four decades would be his glory.

He had been nothing more than a deckhand when he had first sighted this shore from the railing of a merchant ship. He had brought nothing with him but a strong back, a keen mind, the name of his birthplace, SwanSea, and a terrible burning within him. A burning that wouldn't let him rest until he had obliterated all memories of the dank, frigid Welsh coal mines where he had labored as a boy.

In a month he would wed Leonora Spencer, a young woman he had chosen with meticulous care for her breeding and social connections. They would be married here at SwanSea in the immense ball-room that seventy-five florists would turn into a bower. Leonora would wear diamonds in her hair and on her gown. Special trains would run between New York and Boston, carrying their guests. From Boston, a convoy of coaches would bring them to SwanSea. Society would be talking about this wedding for years.

He was pleased. The marriage would not only ac-complish the feat of bringing society to his door-step, but Leonora would also provide him with sons.

Without warning, a cloud skimmed across the sun, blunting the light that had been shining on the house, turning its stone cold and its windows dull and opaque. A chill shuddered through Edward. No, he thought. *No.* This wasn't right. Deprived of the sun's golden warmth, the house had no heart, no life; it looked like a mausoleum.

Leonora had said much the same thing when she had first seen the house. For some reason, when she gazed at the house, she couldn't see what he saw. But he was confident that with time she would. Once the house was filled with furniture, art, and guests, it would be everything he had ever dreamed it could be. As if to prove his point, the cloud passed on, and the full strength of the sun's light poured over the house again. Edward felt soothed. Everything would be as he planned.

He had made his fortune. Now he would establish his name. His destiny would be his children. He would give them the best of everything, and in return, they would make their marks in business, politics, and academia. Society would open their arms to him and his family. Presidents would come to him for advice.

From SwanSea he would launch a dynasty that the world would come to respect, if not revere. Through SwanSea and his children, he would live forever.

One   *The Present Day*

She stood with her back to the ocean, her gaze on the great house before her. *SwanSea*. Caitlin Deverell smiled. She'd been born in this house, lived her first six years here. During that time and when she'd visited in the years since, she'd always had the house pretty much to herself. But now, painters, plasterers, artisans, and gardeners swarmed in and around it.

Her great-grandfather Edward had had the dream and built SwanSea. Her grandfather Jake had made SwanSea a legend. The walls of the house had seen birth and death, pain and joy, love and hate. The bright and the beautiful, the famous and the infamous had all passed through its doors. But to Caitlin it had always been home.

Now after a long sleep, Swansea was reawakening. And she felt a thrill of pride that under her care and direction, SwanSea would be restored to its former splendor and glamour.

Caitlin lifted her face to the sun-warmed ocean breeze. It lingered around her to tease the skirt of her sundress, lifting the hem then sending it rippling in sensuous undulations against her legs. Traveling on, the wind softly embraced the house before rustling through the majestic pines that lay just beyond.

The sun, the wind, the ocean, and SwanSea. Caitlin sighed with contentment, thinking there was a rightness about the day, a sense that all was in its proper place.

Then, unexpectedly, a cloud scudded across the sun, and the wind shifted. Catching a flicker of movement in her peripheral vision, she turned, and immediately her attention was arrested by a tall man who was approaching.

He moved with controlled grace that would have reminded her of a natural athlete if it wasn't for the slightest hint of stiffness in his gait. Black jeans molded his long legs, and a lightweight white sweater stretched across his broad chest. The casual outfit took on an elegance that made it seem as if the jeans and sweater had been designed especially for him. Unable to look away, Caitlin stared, rapt by the strong aura of earthy sensuality radiating from the man. The thought flitted through her mind to wonder what it would be like to be made love to by him.

And still she had no sense of anything out of place.

He stopped in front of her, and the sensation that he was dominating all the space around her came over her suddenly. *Odd.* His thick coal-black hair and pale olive skin drew her gaze; his strong-jawed face interested her; his dark brown eyes riveted her. *Unusual.*

"Caitlin Deverell?"

She'd been so caught up with her thoughts about him that the sound of his deep voice nearly made her jump. "Yes?"

"I'm Nico DiFrenza. A man named Haines said I'd find you here."

"Mr. Haines is my foreman."

Without taking his eyes off her, he indicated the house with a movement of his head. "It has an amazing strength to it."

She stared at him, taken aback yet strangely pleased to hear from a stranger something she'd always felt. "I know."

"Yes, I suppose you do." The walk out to the bluff had taken more out of him than he had expected, Nico realized, and looking at Caitlin Deverell while in his weakened condition wasn't helping. Her eyes were an unusual green tinted by flecks of gold, and he felt the potent effect of them to his spine. Outlined against the vivid blue sky, with the wind blowing her cinnamon-colored hair and the skirt of her gold sundress, she was beautiful. He wondered why he hadn't anticipated the impact she might have on him. Not that it mattered.

"Is there something I can do for you, Mr. DiFrenza?"

Another time, another place, the possibilities would be endless, he thought, and in spite of his weariness, a slow smile spread over his face. "Yes, you can do something for me. You can let me stay here for a few days."

She was reflecting on the notion that the sensuality of his smile hadn't been deliberate when the meaning of his words crystallized in her mind. She stared at him blankly. "I beg your pardon?"

Dammit. His approach had been too abrupt. He curled his fingers inward until he had unconsciously made a fist. "I'm sorry. Let me explain. Like practically everyone else in the country, I've heard of SwanSea. Then just recently, I read that you were turning the house into a resort."

"That's true, but it will be months before it will be ready for guests."

Come on, sweetheart. Don't make this hard for me. I'm just not up to it. This time his smile was quick and meant to take her breath away. The slight widening of her eyes told him it had worked. He forced his fingers to relax and slipped his hands into his pockets. "At least hear me out. Please."

She blinked, realizing he said "please" the way another man might caress. Softly. Persuasively. With a certain charm and seductiveness.

"I'm on a leave of absence from my job, and this morning I headed up the coast."

"That's all very interesting, but—"

"You're not listening."

"Sorry." In the next moment she fought back the urge to laugh. Why was *she* apologizing? He was the trespasser.

"My heart is set on a room with an ocean view, and under ordinary circumstances, I'm sure I wouldn't have any trouble getting one. But there's an insurance convention in Portland, and all the really good places are taken."

"So you thought you could stay here?" She smiled with regret. "No, I'm afraid not. Look, Mr. DiFrenza—"

"Please call me Nico, Miss Deverell."

With a toss of her head, she sent shining cinnamon strands flying behind her shoulders. Nico followed the motion with a concentration that gave her pause. She'd probably tossed her head in that way thousands of times in her twenty-six years, but no man had ever narrowed his eyes at the gesture in quite the same way as Nico had. It was almost as if her action had caused some inner disturbance in him. A funny little shiver went up her spine. She wrapped her arms around her waist. "It's a shame that you couldn't find anything to suit you, but you can't stay here."

His dark brown eyes warmed with a smile, and Caitlin realized that she had never met a man who knew how to smile in so many ways. But she wasn't sure if she'd seen a sincere smile from him yet.

"I've tried one place after another, and I'm tired of driving. A little while ago, when I realized how close I was to SwanSea, I decided it was an omen." His glance darted to the house. "As I said, I really had my heart set on an ocean view." He felt guilty, deceiving her like this, but he had to stay at SwanSea.

She turned toward the sea, giving herself time to think. Up to this moment, she'd thought all the truly compelling men were in her family. But this man . . . He intrigued her. He attracted her. He definitely made her want to do as he asked. She sighed. She couldn't.

She looked back at him and was surprised by the expression of pain on his face. In the next instant, the expression passed, and she decided she had been mistaken. "I suggest that you drive back to the little town you passed on your way here. There's a lovely tearoom there. Have something to eat, then drive on up the coast. I'm sure you'll find something to your liking."

He shook his head, his impatience barely restrained. "Surely you have a room somewhere that I can use, perhaps in a section of the house where the workmen haven't yet started."

She did. On the northwest side of the house on the third floor, where she was staying. "You don't give up, do you?"

"Hardly ever."

She swallowed against a thickness in her throat. The dark intensity of his gaze was stirring up warm quivering sensations inside her that threatened to push aside her common sense. "What you're asking is impossible."

"Nothing," he said, "is impossible."

"It is, Mr. DiFrenza, if I say it is."

So there was steel beneath the beauty, he thought, and silently applauded her. A woman in her circumstances should be cautious. Except in this particular instance when her caution stood in his way.

He ran his hand along his waist to his side and felt the tenderness. For a moment, he struggled with himself. Under normal circumstances, he would never expose a weakness—but in this case, he might be able to use it to his advantage. "I haven't been entirely honest with you, Miss Deverell. I told you I'd taken a leave of absence from work. What I didn't say is that I've been ill . . ."

"Oh, I'm sorry."

As he had hoped, her guard began to melt away, to be replaced by sympathy. He nodded. "I was discharged from the hospital yesterday after being advised that I might recuperate better away from Boston."

Curious though she was, good manners kept her from asking the nature of his illness. But she failed to imagine what could have put him in the hospital. Even with the faint pallor beneath his olive skin, he exuded an astonishing power. It made her wonder what he'd be like when he was entirely well. And, a small voice whispered, if she gave him a room, she'd find out.

In truth, letting him have a room for a few days would cause her very little inconvenience. SwanSea had over fifty bedrooms. And though it was true she knew nothing about him, she also wouldn't know anything about most of the people who would be arriving to stay when SwanSea officially opened. Still, her instincts told her that none of those guests would come close to moving her in this strange, inexplicable way. "I've been living in Boston in recent years. Maybe we know some of the same people."

Only an inherent self-discipline kept him from groaning aloud. She was going to probe. Why did she have to be beautiful *and* smart? "Boston is a big town, I doubt it."

She persevered. "There's a wonderful family-owned department store in Boston by the name of DiFrenza's. Are you by any chance related to the owners?"

He hesitated. He had a circle of close and trusted friends. Outside that circle, he didn't talk about himself. Protecting his family was his first priority, but he had to stay at SwanSea, and to do so, he had to gain Caitlin Deverell's confidence. "Elena DiFrenza is my great-grandmother."

Her eyes widened. "She's a legend in Boston."

"She deserves to be a legend," he said, gratified to see Caitlin relaxing. "She's a remarkable woman."

That Elena DiFrenza was his great-grandmother was reassuring, and it was a fact easily checked. But a doubt Caitlin couldn't quite name continued to niggle at her. "I understand DiFrenza's is about to open a second store in Beverly Hills."

"That's right."

"I shop quite often at DiFrenza's. Are you in the family business?"

"No. In general, I leave the store to my father and my sister. My father heads the store, and my sister is a buyer."

Studying him, Caitlin at first found it difficult to put this obviously rugged man together with the delicate Angelica DiFrenza. Through her frequent patronage of the store, Caitlin had struck up a casual friendship with Angelica, and she often relied on the woman's impeccable taste when she needed something to wear for a special event.

"I know your sister," she said, "and you look nothing alike." Then it struck her. While it was true that Angelica's waist-length hair was dark brown, not coal-black like his, they had the same eyes. Some people called that particular dark-brown shade and velvety texture *bedroom* eyes. Now why was she thinking that?

"I guarantee that Angelica would hate it if she resembled me," he said. Though his words were meant as a joke, his patience was thinning by the minute. "And I wouldn't take it too kindly if I looked like her. Anyway, Mother Nature knew what she was doing when she created Angelica. She's just about perfect."

"She is lovely," Caitlin agreed, reflecting that he was saying all the right things. Why then did she continue to sense something irregular and uneven beneath his smooth manner? Something that made her want to keep digging. "Your sister wears a ring I've always admired."

He'd be amused if it weren't for the fact that he was suddenly so tired. "Yes, it's a Colombian square-cut emerald. Her birthstone." He felt the slight tremor in his limbs. Giving a silent, crude curse, he whipped out his billfold and held out his driver's license for her inspection.

A quick look showed her a stern, unsmiling picture of him and informed her that his name was Niccolo DiFrenza, that he lived at a good address in Boston, that he was six feet tall and had brown eyes.

On a certain level, she was reassured. Everything checked. But on another level, something told her Nico DiFrenza couldn't be so simply and neatly explained by fitting him into a slot on the DiFrenza family tree. There was nothing simple or neat about this man.

"Look, Miss Deverell, please reconsider about the room. I really don't think I can drive one more mile."

His pallor *had* increased, she noticed with concern. "It's just that I'm not sure this is the best place for you. We aren't set up to offer any service. Ramona, my mother's housekeeper, is with me helping out, but all the workers you see are involved in the renovations."

"So you do have other people staying here?"

"I phrased that poorly. Only Ramona and I are actually staying here. The workers come in from the surrounding towns each morning."

"I wouldn't expect room service or someone to bring me fresh towels and make up my bed in the morning. All I need is a bed. Period."

"And an ocean view." She turned slightly to look at the house. "Well, thanks to my great-grandfather Edward Deverell and his Art Nouveau seashell-shaped design, there aren't many rooms in the house that don't have an ocean view."

He saw that she was softening and pressed his advantage. "I promise I won't be a bother. I'll even drive into the town you mentioned for my meals."

"Ramona would have a fit," she said dryly. "As soon as she found out you're recovering from an illness, you'd be lucky if she'd let you lift your own glass of water."

"Then I can stay?"

She was tempted to say yes, but in the end, caution ruled. Reluctantly, she shook her head. "No. But I will give you a bed for a few hours so you can rest before you start out again." He accepted her verdict in stony silence. "All right?" she asked.

"That would be very kind of you."

• • •

Nico stepped back to allow Caitlin to precede him through the massive carved black-walnut front doors, then followed her into the grand entry hall with its forty-foot ceiling and majestic staircase that climbed a story, then branched in opposite directions to climb another story.

Nico lifted his gaze to the top of the stairs and inhaled sharply at the sight of the twenty-foot stained-glass window there, crafted in vibrant greens, purples, golds, and blues.

"Louis Comfort Tiffany designed the window to represent a peacock's head and body," Caitlin offered. "And the marble mosaic of the landing and stairway below it portray the tail."

Nico's gaze followed the vivid plumage of the peacock's tail as it fanned out in the breathtaking jewel-colors of the window to spread down the stairs to the hall floor. "The staircase is a work of art," he said, his voice hushed.

She nodded, pleased with his reaction. "The whole house is." She cast a glance at his pale face. "I forgot to ask you about your bags. Will you need them to freshen up?"

"Probably. They're in my car. I'll get them later."

"Fine." She gazed at him worriedly. He really didn't look at all well. "I think we'd better take the elevator."

His lips compressed. "I can manage the stairs."

Without a word, she took his arm and led him to one of the two gilded elevators tucked beneath the stairway. On the third floor, they walked down a wide hall.

If he were going to be allowed to stay only a few hours, he had to make the best of the time, Nico thought, trying to focus on the layout of the house. But all the doors that led off the hall were closed, and he couldn't summon his usual excellent sense of direction. "Is your room on this floor?"

"Yes, I'm a few doors down from the one I'm lending you, and Ramona's room is at the end of the hall. Traditionally, the family's private rooms are on this floor, but I'm planning on converting a series of suites on the fourth floor into rooms to be used exclusively for the family. That will give us more privacy, and we'll always have rooms available when we want to come and stay."

His strength dwindling rapidly now, Nico stared down at the Persian carpet, concentrating on putting one foot after the other. He had to learn the general arrangement of the place, he told himself, but later. For now, rest was the top priority.

She stopped in front of a door and opened it. "I put this room in order in case my mother decides to drop in."

He threw an unseeing glance around the large room. "Are you expecting her anytime soon?"

"I never know. Mother's a restless soul, and she travels a great deal."

He noticed a slight edge in her voice, but he didn't look at her face. He focused on the big bed, its tall headboard done in marquetry work of dark stained wood with inlaid ivory and mother-of-pearl. He crossed to it and eased himself down onto the cream-colored satin coverlet.

She walked to the French windows and opened them. "I'm not sure where my mother is at the moment. She has homes in both Paris and Boston, but the last postcard I received from her had a picture of the Great Pyramid of Giza on it." A tiny frown creased her forehead. "No telling where she is now." She swept her hand in an arc before her. "Well, there it is. An ocean view, as ordered." Turning, she found him sprawled on the bed, asleep.

She stared at him for a moment. Against the pale

satin coverlet, his features seemed harder, his skin darker, his whole being more sensual and masculine. Like granite against silk, the contrast brought out the best of both.

She slowly shook her head, bewildered. She didn't think she'd ever had such a strong reaction to a man, and she couldn't explain it. But for some reason, she wasn't particularly bothered.

She pulled a blanket from the wardrobe. At his side, she started to bend over him with the cover but then stopped. His sweater had separated from the waistband of his jeans, and the lower part of a large bandage had been exposed. Immediately her heart went out to him. He hadn't been lying when he said he'd been ill. Actually it appeared that he'd either sustained some sort of injury or that he had had surgery. Speculation aside, whatever had been wrong with him, he'd obviously been through the mill.

With special care, she spread the cover over him, bringing it up to his chin. Straightening, she looked down at him. Exhausted though he obviously was, he still managed to maintain a certain wariness, a measure of control, even in sleep. There was no doubt about it. She was fascinated by him.

To be held spellbound by a powerful attraction could be dangerous. But it could also be exciting, pleasurable, fulfilling.

What was she going to do about it, she wondered.

Still half asleep, Nico stretched. Pain in his side brought him wide awake to a dark room. A check of the luminescent dial on his watch informed him that he'd been asleep four hours. Damn. He had meant only to rest, not fall asleep.

He tried to recall what had happened. He remembered lying down, he remembered Caitlin walking to the window . . . Her voice . . . Her graceful movements . . .

He rubbed a hand over his face. He couldn't allow her to distract him. Swiftly he went over what he knew about her. Since earning her B.A. from Harvard, she'd held an executive position with Deverell, Incorporated, the family business in Boston that was run by her cousin, Conall Deverell, a shark of a businessman. She had an uncle who was chairman of the board of the company, another uncle who was a powerful United States senator. A third uncle had died a hero in the Korean War. Last year, she'd inherited SwanSea from her grandfather Jake Deverell, the distinguished diplomat and statesman. She had beauty, wealth, social position—and SwanSea. In poker that would be called an almost unbeatable hand. Fortunately, he was very good at playing poker.

Mindful of his wound, he carefully reached for the switch on the bedside lamp. As he sat up, a blanket slid off him, and he saw his two bags sitting on the floor beside the bed. The idea that someone had been in his room while he slept fired him to action.

He checked his bags to make sure nothing had been disturbed, then stripped off his sweater and jeans. In the bathroom, he flipped on the light and discovered a stack of thick white towels and washcloths piled beside a black-marble basin with gold faucets in the shape of swans' heads. Nice, very nice.

The house was astonishing, and its mistress . . .

Looking into the mirror at himself, he shook his head. *No, Nico. No.*

Deliberately, he dropped his gaze to the two large gauze-pads on the left side of his upper body, one over his ribs, the other below his heart. He peeled off the bandages and studied the healing wounds, a grim expression on his face. He supposed he should be grateful that Nathan Rettig hadn't been a better shot. A half inch more to the right and one of the bullets would have punctured his heart. As it was, the first bullet had grazed a rib, and the second had nicked his spleen. The result had been two hellish weeks in the hospital, with only policemen to keep him company.

He owed Rettig, Nico thought, and he was going to see that he was paid off in spades.

"Hello," Caitlin said as Nico walked into the kitchen. She was sitting at the big walnut table in the center of the large room, drinking coffee. And until she saw him, she hadn't admitted to herself that she'd been waiting for him. "You're looking a little better."

"I feel better," he said honestly. He'd showered and changed into another pair of black jeans, along with a long-sleeved blue-and-black-striped shirt. He'd left the collar open and rolled up the sleeves to his forearms.

Sexy, she thought, then caught herself. "Next time you tell me you need a room, I'll respond very quickly."

The teasing glints in the green-gold eyes caused a tingling along his nerves. He ignored the sensation. "Sorry to conk out on you like that, but I guess the drive took more out of me than I realized."

"Don't apologize. I understand."

I hope not, he thought. "By the way, my bags were in the room when I woke, and I was wondering who brought them in."

The wariness in his seeemingly casual question brought her head up. "I did."

He concentrated on excluding all tightness from his expression. "Does that mean I can stay?"

The answer was on the tip of her tongue, but she forced herself to consider the situation one more times. She folded her hands on the table in front of her and stared at them for a moment. He was already here. She'd taken his bags upstairs herself. And there was her incredible fascination. *I've got to be crazy.* "I'd hate to see you have to start out this time of night and try to find a place."

"Is that a yes?"

She met his gaze. "I guess it is."

"Thank you," he said allowing himself to relax a degree. "The please call me Nico."

"Fine, if you'll call me Caitlin."

Caitlin. The sound of her name rebounded softly through his brain, hitting all sorts of pleasure sensors. But then he remembered. It wouldn't pay to get too close or to become obligated to the people in this house. His plan was to get in, spend some time, accomplish his tasks, and get back out. Smooth. Without causing a ripple. "I meant it when I said I don't intend to be a bother."

A small smile lifted her lips. "I know, and believe me, I don't have time to wait on you. But as it happened, it was no trouble for me to bring up the bags. Now, why don't you sit down, and I'll get your dinner."

"Dinner?"

The two men she'd been closest to in her life, Jake and Conall, were both formidable men with wide streaks of stubbornness and pride, so the objection Nico was about to make didn't deter her. She pushed away from the table and stood up. "Ramona made a huge casserole for the two of us tonight, and there was quite a bit left over. She left it warming for you."

She grabbed a hot pad, bent to pull the dish from the oven, and set it on the counter, talking all the while to distract him. "Remodeling this kitchen is going to be a hellish job. I really dread it. But in order to hold the type of up-to-date professional equipment we'll need for the resort, we're going to have to rearrange the kitchen and knock out a couple of walls to make it large enough. That one"—she pointed to a wall—"and the one beyond that. We'll lose the original servants' dining hall, but there are so many other rooms down here that we can connect into a dining room and lounge for our employees, we won't even miss it."

"Caitlin."

The sound of his iron-hard voice made her turn and look at him. "Yes?"

"I won't allow Ramona or you to go to extra trouble for me."

She shrugged. "You'll have to take that up with Ramona. I never tell her what to do." She scooped a large portion of the casserole onto a plate and set it in front of him, along with a basket of hot, crusty French bread.

"Beef bourguignonne?" he asked.

"Yes. Coffee?"

He nodded, thinking that there probably weren't a lot of people who would call beef bourguignonne a casserole, but his brief glimpses of the house had already begun to teach him that there were the rich, and then there were the *rich*.

Ignoring the food, he watched Caitlin as she moved around the room. Unfortunately he couldn't find a thing about her to fault. The sundress left her arms, throat, and back bare and revealed skin the color of ivory with a tantalizing undertone of gold. She was too damned beautiful for his peace of mind.

"Did you have any trouble finding the kitchen?"

He shrugged. "A little. I took the elevator down to the first floor, then headed in the general direction of the back of the house. It should have been simple, but it wasn't. I had no idea how huge this place is until I made a few wrong turns. And it hadn't occurred to me that the kitchen would be in the half-basement." He took the cup of coffee from her outstretched hand and waited until she sat down again. Now was as good a time as any, he thought, to get a little information. Mainly, though, it would give him something else to think about beside her—something he badly needed. "What's the general layout of the place?"

There was a coiled alertness in him that seemed to have come out of nowhere, and it presented her with a moment's unease. She wondered if his controlled energy was natural, or if it came and went with each new difficult situation. No, she thought. This wasn't a difficult situation, and it was normal that he would want to learn how to get around the place where he'd be staying for a few days. She was being too suspicious. She smiled. "Knowing the layout would make it easier for you, wouldn't it?"

He nodded, his gaze dropping to the fullness of her curving mouth. She wore no lipstick, but a delicate sheen of moisture had been applied to the natural soft pink color of her lips. He'd like to kiss his way through that sheen of moisture to the taste and the texture beneath. A strong surge of hunger shook him; he picked up his fork and tried hard to dredge up interest in the beef bourguignonne.

"Okay, I'll give you a rundown on the highlights. Here in the half-basement there's the kitchen, its pantries, which are quite extensive, service and storage rooms, and the servants' dining hall. On the first floor, there's the great hall and staircase, of course, and all the formal rooms. The drawing rooms, a banquet hall, a smaller dining room, plus a library and the study are also on the first floor."

To his disgust, he was having trouble keeping his mind on business. He was finding Caitlin infinitely more absorbing than the information she was giving him, and he had to have the information. So far, nothing had worked out as he had planned. No, that wasn't true. His first objective had been accomplished. He was now an official guest at SwanSea. He'd just have to come to terms with this incredible attraction he had for Caitlin. He *had* to, because he wasn't sure ignoring her would be possible. "Study? That was your grandfather . . . Jake's study?"

"That's right, and it was also Edward's. The ballroom, a billiard room, a music room, and more sitting rooms are on the second floor. I'm going to turn most of those sitting rooms into meeting areas. The third floor contains bedrooms, dressing rooms, and sitting rooms, as does the fourth floor. Neither the third nor fourth floor has enough bathrooms or closets, so dressing rooms and some sitting rooms will be converted for those two relatively modern conveniences."

"What about the attic?"

"Storage and servants' quarters. One of these days soon, I've got to get around to going through all the trunks and boxes up there."

Interest quickened in him. "You don't know what's stored there?"

"Some of it I do. I used to play up there as a child. But a great many new things have only recently been transferred to the attic from rooms currently being worked in."

"I'm surprised you didn't store it."

"All the really valuable items *are* in storage. And a

lot of the furniture has been sent off to refinishers. A first-floor sitting room, the study, and the bedrooms on the third floor are practically the only rooms left with all of their furniture."

Having gotten a few of the answers he needed, he finished eating, then leaned back in the chair to study Caitlin. He could afford the luxury just this once, he assured himself. After all, greater knowledge could help him deal with her.

She was a woman who had had the best of everything all her life. She could coast through life on her beauty alone, not to mention her wealth, but by all accounts, she could have become a vital part of the Deverell organization if she'd stayed. Instead, she'd taken on a new and different challenge. "I'm curious. What made you decide to turn this place into a resort?"

She smoothed her thumb and finger around the porcelain rim of her coffee cup, a gesture that unexpectedly brought life to his lower limbs and made him shift uncomfortably in his chair.

"In college, I'd majored in business because it seemed like the thing to do at the time, and it was relatively easy for me. When I graduated, I *naturally*" —she grinned, giving the emphasized word significance and charm—"went to work at Deverell's. I was in the public relations department, and I'd begun to feel restless when I inherited SwanSea."

"Restless about where you were in the company?" he asked, totally engrossed in what she was saying.

"No. Public relations wasn't the problem. I could have worked in any department I chose, including assisting Conall, my cousin. But I had found a certain confinement and rigidity to the business world that had begun to chafe."

"Even in a company where you must have had a certain amount of power?"

"Yes, because I would never have abused that power."

Somehow he'd known that, he thought.

"Your family must have hated the idea of you turning your back on the business." His had, in spades. The fights between him and his father had been terrible.

"They called me crazy at first," she admitted. "They couldn't see the practicality. But they have their own warm feelings for SwanSea, and now they can't wait for the grand opening."

"But running SwanSea will be a business too."

The sudden luminosity of her expression caught him unaware and caused a tightening in his gut.

"Yes, but SwanSea is different somehow. This place has been a part of me all my life. It was my first home. And even after my mother and I left and lived in Boston, I always considered myself a part of it. I know exactly what's right for it, and I've thought things through very carefully. The style of life Edward Deverell had in mind when he built the place is no longer practical. When I inherited SwanSea, I had several options, one being to open it for tours. But it would have been too dispassionate to have groups of tourists tramping through its rooms."

"Dispassionate?"

She grinned. "You probably think that's a funny way to speak of a house, but I can't be unemotional when it comes to SwanSea. Remember? You noticed its strength. The house is almost a living force."

He nodded, recalling the strange feeling that had come over him at his first glimpse of the house. It had seemed to have a rhythmic energy. Even more strange, it had seemed to be welcoming him. He'd chalked up the reaction to his weariness.

Then there had been his reaction to Caitlin. As

much as he had tried to ignore it, he had been strongly attracted to her. He hadn't expected that with simply a look, a gesture, or a smile, she could make his insides catch fire. He'd slept, awakened rested, and found he still wanted her.

The burning she saw in his eyes gave her momentary pause, a burning that singed her to her fingertips. But was the heat really there? she wondered, or was she seeing something she wanted to see?

"I also decided against giving SwanSea to the government or the state." Her lips twisted wryly. "The truth is, I'm selfish. The romantic side of me wants always to be able to call SwanSea home, to come and stay whenever I want, to have a part in its future; and hopefully in the years ahead, my children will take over for me. The practical side of me wants to see that SwanSea is preserved, but preserved in such a way that it's not simply another sideshow or an empty monument. By turning it into a resort, I'll be able to control what happens to it for as long as I live." She stopped, no longer able to doubt the expression in Nico's dark brown eyes. The look was a sensual wanting that left her weak.

"You're quite a lady, Caitlin Deverell," he said softly. "Romantic *and* practical. You've figured out how to safeguard and protect the house and, at the same time, how to give it back its life."

"SwanSea deserves loving attention. This is a gracious house, and I want to give other people the opportunity to come to know SwanSea the way I do, to stay here for however long they can, to rest, to draw energy from its atmosphere, to love and be happy within its walls."

He gave a short laugh, attempting to break free of the web of desire that bound him tighter with her every word, his every breath. "I guess it's a good thing I'm seeing the house now. When it opens, I probably wouldn't be able to afford to stay."

She frowned, taking his lighthearted words seriously. "I wish we weren't going to have to charge so much, but I'm afraid the value of SwanSea's contents along with the high costs for renovation, insurance, upkeep, and staff dictate high prices. The resort will be *very* exclusive, but that's the compromise I've had to make to accomplish the things I want." Suddenly a puzzled look came over her face. "What do you mean you couldn't afford to stay here. What about DiFrenza's?"

"My family's business, not mine." He gave her a smile meant to divert. "I forgot to ask how much you're going to charge me, didn't I?"

Feeling a warmth in the pit of her stomach, she returned his smile. "Yes, but I wouldn't worry about it. With SwanSea so far from being finished, I can guarantee your bill will be very affordable."

"You have quite a task in front of you."

"It's a labor of love. SwanSea is one of the best surviving examples of Art Nouveau in America. Everything, from the design of the house to the door handles, panelings and moldings creates a unity." Suddenly she had to swallow against a dry throat. Unable to go on any further, even about a subject she loved so much, she sat back, aroused, excited, and unsettled. She was used to the passion she felt for her birthplace, but the turbulence Nico had created within her was something she wasn't sure how to cope with. She tried again. "I'm really sorry you're not seeing the house at its best. You'll have to promise to come back when the restoration and renovations are completed." She gave a husky, uncertain laugh. "I'll give you a special rate."

He heard her uncertainty and understood she was

drawn to him. He had far too much experience not to know that with a little effort he could have her. He shifted restlessly in his chair. The idea played with his mind, seducing him.

He brought his thoughts to a halt. If there was one thing he'd learned over the years, it was that hardly anything was simple and straightforward or what it seemed. Caitlin obviously hadn't learned that lesson yet, and he wasn't sure how he felt about being the one to teach her. There was an openness and a warmhearted quality about her—the complete opposite of himself.

Damn this edginess, he thought angrily. Coming here *had* seemed like the perfect plan. "I think I'd better call it a night."

It was a shock for Caitlin to realize she didn't want Nico to go. In her twenty-six years, she'd been through the normal ups and downs with men that most women of her age experience. But the strong, instant response to him was unique. He had made no advances to her, but a look from him was as potent as a kiss from any other man she'd known. Involuntarily, her gaze was drawn to his lips. They were strong and firm, and he would know exactly how to use them on a woman. "I'll go up with you, to make sure you have everything you need."

He closed his eyes against the sight of her, but he couldn't close down the functioning of his brain, and his imagination sprang into overdrive. What would it be like to reach across the table, pull her onto its top, and climb over and into her? Heaven, his body told him. Heaven.

He stood so quickly he bumped the table. The plates rattled, and an empty glass toppled over, then rolled off the table and crashed to the floor. The sound of the shattering glass was earsplitting in an atmosphere of aroused senses. "It's not necessary to come up with me. I have what I need, and I can find my own way."

Disappointed, she walked around the table and reached for his plate.

"I'll get it," he murmured and brushed her hand as he too reached for the plate.

Her gaze locked with his, and for a moment, Caitlin forgot everything but the strange aching need in her. "I'm just trying to help, Nico."

Lord, but her eyes were beautiful, he thought, even with the slight glint of hurt he saw in them. "I know," he whispered and wondered why he felt he was fighting the inevitable. He lifted his hand, intending to touch her cheek, but quickly dropped it to his side before he could brush the inviting softness. "It's just that I'm not used to being waited on."

"You live alone then?" It was a question she should have asked sooner. But then again, she couldn't believe his heart could belong to another—not with the hungry way he looked at her.

"Yes." He wasn't sure, but he didn't think he'd ever wanted to kiss a woman as badly as he wanted to kiss Caitlin. To lick, bite, and taste her until he was sated. To take her, fill her, empty himself into her. And then do it again.

The tantalizing scent of her skin floated into his brain, momentarily blocking caution. This time he touched her as he lightly stroked his fingers across one bare shoulder. Velvet. The urge to crawl inside her scented velvet skin was almost overpowering.

He closed his hand around her arm and pulled her against him. Everywhere her soft, curving body touched his, he felt heat. A muscle clenched in his jaw. He was going to take her.

In the next instant, he released her, unsure why.

Sanity. Training. A sense of self-preservation.

Whatever the reason, he was intensely grateful—and fiercely disappointed. "Good night, Caitlin."

"Good night."

A few minutes later, in his room, he carefully settled himself on the bed and covered his eyes with his forearm. Maybe if he couldn't see, he wouldn't be able to think. And if he couldn't think, he wouldn't be able to remember. But his senses were working overtime, and he could still feel her skin against his fingertips.

Damn whatever this thing was between him and Caitlin. Something in him ignited whenever he came near her, and she obviously felt the same way. It was almost as if each of them had exactly the right elements within them to strike sparks off each other. But sparks led to fire, and fire led to danger.

Slowly he lowered his arm. He couldn't let anything happen between them. No matter how much he wanted it. No matter how much she wanted it.

He was in no position to get involved with anyone right now, much less Caitlin Deverell. He just had to keep reminding himself: Caitlin wasn't the reason he was here.

And when the pain came and he couldn't sleep, he told himself it was from his wounds, not from wanting her.

Two

Lord, how she'd wanted Nico to kiss her last night, Caitlin remembered as she left the elevator on the first floor the next morning. She'd wanted it so much that when he'd told her good-night, she'd felt as if he'd inflicted a wound deep within her.

Nice going, Caitlin, she told herself, *and so much for all your caution.* She clicked her tongue in disgust. She should have saved herself a lot of time and trouble and agreed to let him stay as soon as he'd asked her the first time. And then, after all her turmoil, she'd spent most of her night trying to put yesterday and Nico DiFrenza into perspective.

She'd been spectacularly unsuccessful.

All her instincts were telling her that there was more to him than met the eye. Secrets. Parts that he wasn't showing. But deep inside, she felt a powerful pull toward him that she didn't understand and couldn't seem to fight.

A new feeling sparkled inside her, a feeling that was part excitement, part dread. She felt as if she were holding a hand grenade, and she wasn't sure who held the pin: she or Nico.

She sighed loudly, unaware that more than one stare followed her, curious at her unusual self-absorption. She felt nothing but impatience with the day's work that awaited her, but her list of things to do was long, and the first order of business was to speak with her foreman. She found him supervising several workers in the main drawing room. A huge room, it involved painstaking work to restore the original Art Nouveau style of the elegant swirling movements in the wood, metal, and marble surfaces.

"How are things going, Mr. Haines?"

"Fine, Mistress Caty. Just fine."

His response brought her back to the reality at hand, and she hid a smile. Jeb Haines, a tall man with steel-blue eyes and a shock of gray hair tucked under a cap, had lived all his life in the small town five miles beyond the gates of SwanSea. Like so many of the men who were working here now, he had known her almost from the first day of her life. Mistress Caty had been his pet name for her, and he was a man set in his ways. But she didn't mind. The continuity of SwanSea and the people around it comforted her. "No problems?"

"Not any more than what you'd normally expect." He squinted at a young man perched high on a ladder, who was methodically and patiently stripping away several layers of varnish from the carved molding. "You take care up there, Richie. That molding was here before you were born, and if you treat it right, it'll be here after you're gone, too."

Richie threw the older man a grin. "You worry too much. Morning, Miss Deverell."

"Morning, Richie." She turned back to Jeb Haines. "He's right. You do worry too much. But I can't tell you how much I appreciate the conscientious work you're doing."

He lifted his hat, smoothed his hair, and replaced the hat. "Well now, I guess I do worry. But you know, this house is one of my earliest memories. I was a young boy during the times of your grandfather, Jake, God rest his soul. And your grandmother, Arabella—my, my, but she was a high-spirited lady. Me and my friends all had crushes on her, and we weren't the only ones, let me tell you."

Caitlin grinned. "That's what I've heard."

"Well, you heard right. And this house fairly glittered when they lived here. You can't see the house from town, but we used to make up all sorts of reasons to come down the road and have a look. 'Course, eventually the house was closed up, but I still loved to look at it. It was like as long as it was here, everything was all right. You know what I mean?"

"I know," she said softly.

"Then when we were building the church—oh, that must have been about twenty-five, twenty-six years ago now—I could see the house from the roof. What a sight that was."

"It must have been," she said, wondering fondly why Jeb Haines had missed the news that New Englanders were supposed to be taciturn. She glanced at her watch. "Conrad Gilbert will be here in about an hour," she said, naming the architect who was working with her on the restoration and conversion of the house. "Can you join us?"

"Just tell me where."

"Probably one of the second-floor sitting rooms. I'll come get you." She paused. "By the way, have you seen a tall black-haired man this morning?"

"Sure have. Said he was staying here."

"That's right."

"I think I saw him going into the study."

"Thank you."

As she strolled slowly toward the study, she told herself that there was no earthly reason why she should be seeking out Nico. As a matter of fact, there were probably several reasons why she shouldn't. But disturbingly erotic thoughts of him had kept her tossing and turning all night. She'd never seen that particular combination of danger, physical weakness, and compelling power in a man before. She wanted to see him, to be near him, *now*.

Knowing very well that she should stay away, she went to him anyway.

She opened the study door and discovered Nico bent over the big desk. When he looked up and saw her, he closed a drawer.

A troubled line creased her brow as she gazed at Nico. With his self-assurance and inherent poise, he seemed to belong behind the desk with its commanding, rhythmic lines and its rich, exotic citron wood. And yet she couldn't shake the sense that he'd been searching for something. "What are you doing?"

With the manner of someone completely worry-free, he straightened and eased a hip down onto the desktop. "Good morning. I expected to see you in the kitchen when I came down, but Ramona told me you usually skipped breakfast."

"Ramona? You've met Ramona?"

"Terrifying lady."

"Terrifying?" Did he really mean that? Ramona had worked for her mother for twenty-four years, and never in all that time had she been frightened of her.

"She wouldn't let me cook. When I tried to insist, she threatened to bring me breakfast in bed tomorrow."

"Yes, I can see why that would terrify you." She

spoke slowly, distractedly. Though his words seemed easy, unforced, she still couldn't help but feel something wasn't quite right.

He shrugged. "I gave in and let her prepare my breakfast."

She crossed the vast expanse of parquet floor to the front of the desk. "What are you doing in here, Nico?"

One dark brow rose. "Oh, I'm sorry. Is this off limits?"

"No, of course not." She looked around the room. The morning sun heightened the golden tones of the furniture, the paneling, and the floor. The overall effect was one of harmony and warmth. She felt neither of those things, but couldn't explain her unease.

Nico cursed silently. Her obvious disquiet at finding him riffling through the desk made guilt twist uncomfortably through him. Guilt was a new emotion to him. He didn't like it, and in this situation, it could be extremely bad. "You don't have a pen I could borrow, do you? I was writing a letter to my great-grandmother, and mine ran out of ink." He walked to a chair and side table by a window and picked up the pen lying across a piece of stationery half-filled with writing. He scratched the pen in circles over the paper, but no ink came out. "I thought maybe there might be a pen in the desk."

Caitlin let out a sigh of relief and hoped he hadn't noticed. How stupid of her to jump to the wrong conclusion. "I don't know about a pen, but there are probably crayons in the desk. I used to spend hours there, drawing pictures."

"What kind of pictures?"

She laughed. "Badly drawn pictures, I can assure you. And to answer your question, no, I don't have a pen, but I keep some in the kitchen. I started out working in my bedroom, then the paper work spilled over into the kitchen. Yesterday, Ramona told me bluntly that I was crowding her out." She laughed lightly. "I'll be moving everything in here tomorrow."

He nodded while carefully phrasing his next words. "I couldn't help but notice the desk was pretty empty. . . ."

"The desk hasn't been used for business in years. All of Jake and Edward's personal papers are stored away."

"Here in the house?"

"For the most part. Just more things I have to go through." She drew a deep breath. Her earlier suspicions had prevented the awkwardness she'd expected after last night. But now she was suddenly uncertain what to say next. "How are you this morning? Did you rest well?"

She was wearing a sleeveless, white, curve-skimming shift that ended above her knees and made the ivory hue of her skin, the green-gold of her eyes, and the cinnamon shade of her hair more vivid, more desirable. "I slept very well," he lied smoothly. "As a matter of fact, I thought I'd take a walk in a little while." What he heard himself say next shocked him. "Could you come with me?"

She hesitated and glanced at her watch. "I have a meeting in about an hour. After that, I'm free."

He told himself that it was only practical to ask her to join him on the walk. For instance, she might drop some small bit of information that he would find useful. "Why don't we meet in the kitchen? Ramona more or less ordered me to come back at about one for lunch. If I don't show up, I'm afraid to think what she might do." His comment was light-hearted, but Caitlin was looking at him with eyes so wide and an expression so serious, he decided he had to smile or kiss her.

His slow smile made her pulse race. *Caitlin, Caitlin, what* are *you doing?* she asked herself.

"Are you getting tired?" she asked, interrupting what she'd been telling him about her plans to convert the carriage house into a guest house.

"No, actually I'm feeling much better than yesterday. It must be the sea air and my ocean view."

She laughed as he had intended. He enjoyed watching her laugh. And he enjoyed watching the way the sun seemed to touch her skin with a gentle golden color. And he just plain enjoyed watching her. It bothered him like hell.

She waved to two gardeners. "In Edward's day, there were over a hundred acres of gardens, all extensively landscaped. It wouldn't be feasible, though, for me to try to reclaim all of the land. Besides, I like the new thickets of pines that have grown up and the meadows of wild flowers that you find in the spring. But at least part of the grounds are on their way back to how they were in Edward's time."

There was that mix of the practical and the romantic, he thought, disconcerted because of how much he was intrigued. "I'm glad you're not going to try to reclaim all of it. Nature's way is usually best, not only for the people but also for the animals. We have quite a few that make their home at my great-grandmother's country house."

"What kind?"

"Oh, deer, squirrels, rabbits, raccoons." The corners of his mouth lifted slightly. "When I was a little boy, I'd spend hours trying to get the deer to eat from my hand."

"Did you succeed?"

"Yes. I had all the patience in the world then. I wonder where that patience went to."

"You don't feed the deer anymore?"

He hesitated, suddenly wondering why he'd even mentioned the deer. "On occasion I try. But if they don't come to me within a reasonable amount of time, I toss the oats where they can see them and leave."

"You know what I think?"

He shifted his weight from one foot to the other, uncomfortable at how easily he'd let this conversation slip out of his control. "I can't imagine."

"I think you might not suffer fools or your own weaknesses easily, but I bet when it counts, you still have patience, especially with people you care about."

He was utterly stunned by her assessment of him. As right as she was, it would be wrong for him to allow her to think too kindly of him. He wanted to snap back a retort, but much to his surprise, his answer held a tinge of sadness. "You don't even know me, Caitlin."

Staring at the sharp angles of his profile, she realized he had a point. But something inside her insisted that she did know him. She wasn't sure she trusted him, but she trusted herself, and being with him felt absolutely right. Nearing the edge of the bluff, she turned so that she faced the sea and the wind.

At any rate, her feelings for him weren't serious. Not yet. The pull might be strong, but they hadn't even kissed. No real damage had been done, she told herself, conveniently forgetting how she'd felt last night.

Inhaling the tang of the salt air, she gazed at the sight before her, a sight almost as familiar to her as her own image in a mirror, one that soothed and calmed. The gray water glistened in the early afternoon sun. A lone fishing boat was silhouetted against the blue sky as it cruised past the island. Seagulls called and circled overhead.

"Who owns the island?" Nico suddenly asked.

"I do. It's part of SwanSea. There's a cottage on it."

"Does anyone live there?"

She shook her head. "When I was little, Mother and I used to sail over and have picnics. I need to check on the place soon."

"Exactly how long has it been since anyone from your family has been out there?"

"Years, probably. Ben Stephenson has been the caretaker here for as long as I can remember. He goes over once in a while, although there's nothing left of any value in the way of furnishings or paintings." She thought for a moment. "But the island is wonderful. I've visited islands all over the world, and I like that one best."

"Why?"

She considered the island with slightly narrowed eyes. "I think all its rocks and pines give it character and a sort of hardy, tough beauty. White sandy beaches and tropical flowers are nice, but—"

"You want more than a pretty postcard picture?"

"Definitely." She gazed up at him. "And what do you want?"

You, naked, beneath me in my bed. The unexpected thought hit him like a blow that was all the more brutal because he hadn't had a chance to prepare a defense.

"What do you mean?" he asked carefully.

"What would you like to see next?"

The answer was the same, he thought achingly.

He had all the normal sexual needs and desires of a healthy male. In the past, he'd always taken care of his body's requirements in a prudent, discreet, and uncomplicated manner with women who understood that affairs were nothing more than a game. But the needs and wants Caitlin made him feel were abnormal in their power, scope, and demand. With her, a recklessness threatened to take over, and that wasn't good. He wanted her, but he couldn't have her, and the whole situation made him mad as hell. "It doesn't matter. Whatever you like."

"Then let's walk over to the tennis courts. I want to check on the progress of the work over there."

"Fine."

She glanced curiously at him, wondering why he suddenly sounded so abrupt. Finding no clue, she followed an impulse and took his hand.

He looked down at the hand she had placed in his. It was probably the most unthreatening gesture that had been made to him in his recent memory, and he found himself wishing he hadn't convinced her to let him stay.

"You know, Caitlin, some people think that Jack the Ripper was a member of the British royal family."

"Yes, so I've heard," she said, startled by his off-the-wall comment.

"The point is, you based your decision to let me stay here on the fact that I'm Elena DiFrenza's great-grandson."

"That was part of the reason," she said slowly.

"You realize, don't you, that I could be her great-grandson and still be an ax murderer in my spare time."

"In your spare time?" Amused, she asked, "Are you?"

"No."

"Then why bring it up?"

Sighing, he scrubbed his free hand over his cheek. "I'm sorry."

Her amusement faded as she realized he'd been serious. "Why would you say something like that, Nico? Tell me. I really want to know."

"Maybe, I was trying to warn you. I'm not an ax murderer, but, Caitlin, I'm a lot of other things that aren't so nice."

"Okay, then. You want to tell me about those other things?"

"No." He pulled his hand from hers. "And as a matter of fact, I think I'll go up to my room and rest for a while."

"I thought you said you weren't tired."

He wasn't, he thought, gazing down at her, feeling the need he'd begun to associate with her pound through his veins. Fortunately, he also felt the control he'd always depended on and a strained but still connected thread of decency. In his line of work, he didn't often encounter the basic sweetness and goodness Caitlin possessed. He had learned that her beauty was both inside and out. She didn't deserve the grief he might bring her, he thought. And, actually, dammit, neither did he.

"You said my being Elena DiFrenza's great-grandson was part of the reason you let me stay here. What was the other part?"

"When you stretched out on the bed yesterday, your sweater pulled up enough that I could see the bottom of your bandage."

"You saw my bandages?"

"Bandages? I saw part of one bandage."

A muscle in his jaw tightened, relaxed, then tightened again. "What else did you see?"

"You," she said softly, "asleep."

Nico read the sensual awareness in her eyes with a sinking heart and a hardening body.

He could not let whatever this was between them blossom.

Unable to prevent it, his gaze dropped to her breasts, and he saw her stiffened nipples outlined against the white bodice. She shouldn't be feeling those things, he thought with despair, even as a corresponding primitive reaction rose up inside him.

Fortunately there was something else. She had her doubts and uncertainties about him. He sensed them, heard them, as if she'd spoken them aloud.

Hold onto your doubts, Caitlin, he silently urged. *They may be your only salvation.*

Something awakened Nico. He tensed, trying to orient himself to his surroundings. Raising up on his elbows, he scanned the darkened room until he was sure he was alone, then collapsed back onto the pillows and drew a hand across his sweat-soaked brow. He had been dreaming of lovely green-gold eyes and ugly copper-and-brass bullets.

Immediately after dinner, he had pleaded fatigue and retired to his room, badly needing distance between Caitlin and himself. Once in bed, he'd fallen into a deep sleep. But now he heard something. . . .

Music. A lilting melody drifted through the open windows and into his room with the night air. What was that tune? It sounded familiar, but he couldn't place it. And who was playing music at—he checked his watch—midnight?

He rolled off the bed, reached for his pants, and dressed so quickly that he left the room without taking time to button his shirt.

Following the music, he made his way through the

halls and rooms of the huge house. He walked through shades of darkness and shadows overlaid by shadows, and he didn't once think of his reasons for coming to SwanSea. It was the music that drew him. Or so he told himself.

Downstairs in one of the drawing rooms, where dustcovers took on the odd shapes of the furniture beneath them, he discovered the source of the music—an old upright Victrola phonograph with a 78-rpm record playing on it. And outside the open doors on the veranda, Caitlin stood at the balustrade.

"Caitlin?"

She turned, her absorbed expression clearing as she saw him. "Hi. What are you doing up?"

"The music woke me."

She looked startled for a moment, then glanced up to his room. "I'm sorry. I didn't even think about being on the same side of the house as your bedroom."

"It's all right." He slid his hands into his pockets and strolled toward her, his gaze roaming intently over her. She was wearing peach satin lounging pajamas, with the legs wide at the bottom, a lacy camisole, and her hair like fire against the overjacket.

She looked too beautiful, too desirable.

He felt too much on edge, too full of desire.

He should return to his room, he thought, and in the next moment gave in to his curiosity. "What are you doing up?"

"Oh, I don't know. It just seems to be one of those nights when I'm finding it hard to go to sleep."

"Do you have many nights like that?"

"Occasionally . . . when the events of the day refuse to be still and rest until the morning."

"That's an interesting way to put it."

Was it? she wondered. Actually, she was too caught up in him to be sure of what she'd said. She had only to cast her eyes to the enticing space between the edges of his unbuttoned shirt to see the fine black hair that covered his chest. And she had only to inhale to breathe in the masculine scent of his flesh. "What about you? Do you ever have trouble sleeping?"

"Not lately," he said, a tinge of self-disgust in his tone. "I put my head on the pillow, and I go out like a light."

She laid her hand on his arm in a gesture of comfort. "It won't last. You'll get better."

He glanced down at her hand, feeling heat from her touch instead of the comfort she'd intended. Casually, he moved his arm and dislodged her hand.

He was trying to do what was right with her. Lord knew he was trying.

"I'm already better," he said. "I've always healed quickly, and I had a feeling that as soon as I could escape from that damned hospital, I'd improve rapidly."

"Escape?"

"A figure of speech." The peach satin of her outfit took on added luster in the silvery moonlight. He reached out one finger and touched the shoulder. Nice. But he was sure that the sensuousness of the material was nothing compared to her skin.

"You know, I haven't asked what you do for a living."

He stilled. After a moment, he said, "I'm a lawyer."

"A lawyer? That's interesting."

"Not as interesting as whatever happened today to worry you so much you can't sleep."

She supposed it would sound strange to him if she told him that since their meeting yesterday, he had begun to dominate her thoughts to the point that the normal course of her life seemed to be altering. It sounded strange, even to her. She settled for part of the truth. "I received another postcard from my mother. This one had the Taj Mahal on the front of it."

"So she's visiting India. Why should that worry you?"

Her mouth twisted with rueful humor. "India doesn't bother me. Neither does Egypt. What does is that she's been flitting from one country to another for years now. She can't seem to stop. It's as if she's searching for something."

"And she's done this for how long?"

"She started at the same time I entered college. We lived in Boston during my school years, and she was there for me. Back then it was just the two of us, along with Ramona, of course. It was only later that she became so restless."

"What about your father?"

"I don't have one."

He nearly came back with a lighthearted comment about how it was biologically impossible not to have a father, but the serious expression on her face kept him silent. He reached out to her, meaning to comfort her as she had tried to comfort him, but with his hand on her arm, her expression changed, and his heart skipped a beat. Desire and need—emotions he'd been attempting to keep banked down inside himself—were plainly written on her face. She wasn't as aware of the possible repercussions as he was. She was simply a woman who wanted a man.

How long had it been since anything had been that simple for him, he wondered, beginning to harden and hurt. And why shouldn't he allow himself the pleasure of basic simplicity where nothing mattered but the two people involved?

Why? he asked himself. Let me tell you why, Nico.

A tremor shuddered through him as he tried to control his unraveling resolve. He had no idea how long his fevered mind had shut out the dull, rhythmic, scratching sound, but he heard her say, "It's the record. I'll get it."

She disappeared through the high-arched doorway into the drawing room, and he eagerly seized the short time she was gone to take himself in hand. But the music began again—slow, melodic, and haunting. And then Caitlin reappeared, bringing her own melodic and haunting qualities into the air surrounding him. He drew in a deep breath and smelled her fragrance and femininity. What could he do? He couldn't stop breathing. Was he destined always to have her scent with him, in his lungs, in his pores?

He concentrated on the music. "What is that song?"

"George Gershwin's 'Someone to Watch Over Me.' It's one of my favorites. My grandfather saw to it that I cut my teeth on Gershwin and Cole Porter. *Literally.*" She laughed softly as she remembered. "He sang songs like 'Isn't It Romantic,' and 'Embraceable You' to me as lullabies, and later, when I was older, he danced me around and around the ballroom to 'Night and Day' and 'Begin the Beguine', with my feet on his."

For years, Jake Deverell's pictures had filled newspapers as he troubleshot one world crisis or another for the government. Nico tried to imagine this powerful, formidable man dancing with his granddaughter while she balanced on his toes. He found he liked the picture. But even more, he liked the image of her in his own arms.

She laughed again, and the silvery sound stroked his spine.

"It was quite a sight, I can tell you. I was such a gawky, awkward young thing."

"You must have been a beautiful child, because you take my breath away as a woman."

Suddenly, inevitably, her body was burning for his touch. "Dance with me," she whispered huskily.

At first he wasn't sure he had understood her. "What?"

She moved to him and put her arms around him. "Dance with me."

A shock of heat ran through him and told him everything he needed to know about why he had been so careful until now to avoid holding her in his arms. Instinctively he had realized how it would be to have her against him. She was satin, sweet-smelling skin, and soft curves. Everything lovely and desirable. And inside he was dying with need for her.

She stared up at him, her head back, the long line of her throat exposed, her hair streaming down her back. He put his arms around her and pulled her closer. Clouds of music and moonlight, drifts of sea breezes—and most of all Caitlin—threatened his common sense. But Nico was beginning to wonder why he was bothering to resist. She wanted him, and he sure as hell wanted her. He was playing with fire, but he had never had a burn that didn't heal. Where was the harm?

Somewhere in the back of Caitlin's mind, she was aware that they weren't dancing. Not that she had really wanted to dance. If she'd had a conscious thought at all, it was that she wanted to learn the feel of his hard lines, strong arms, firm lips. *Him.*

"Nico," she whispered.

Slowly, methodically, he wrapped long silky strands of her hair around his hand until his hand was tight against her scalp and he controlled the position of her head. "Yes," he said. "Yes." Then his mouth came down on hers, and his tongue thrust hotly into her mouth.

She gave herself up to the kiss and to him as a low moan escaped her throat. She'd imagined this kiss, yearned for it, but she wasn't prepared for its reality. His tongue made outrageously intimate forays into her mouth that inundated her senses with new sensations. Her knees threathened to buckle, but he held her tightly to him, so tightly, it seemed that he was trying to make her part of him. The idea didn't frighten her at all.

He parted her satin jacket, then delved beneath the camisole and closed his hand over her breast. She was fuller than he had thought, more perfect. And the rigidity of her nipple thrilled him. He rolled the taut peak between his fingers, thinking he could spend hours lavishing attention on her breasts and nipples and never grow bored. He salivated to have as much of her as possible in his mouth. He could almost taste the honey-sweetness of her now. And she wouldn't protest. This sure knowledge nearly drove him past the edge of reason. But he held on. He wanted both her and reason, and he wasn't yet ready to admit that was impossible.

Passion unfolded in her body and spread, taking possession. His hands and mouth had an extraordinary sureness that brought her nerves alive. He was seducing her with ease, but the moment seemed too right for Caitlin to resist. His actions and his obvious arousal left no doubt that he wanted her.

In a corner of her mind, she realized he completely controlled her. The idea carried excitement with it, yet the steel-hard control he kept over himself bothered her. Still, she skimmed her hand inside his shirt, along the smooth flesh of his back. Muscles rippled beneath her palm, giving her some sense of his strength, making her tremble with passion. A feminine hunger raged within her to touch all of him—every dip and rise of his body, every plane and curve. She wanted to learn him intimately, and she let her hand rove freely, but when she encountered the tape securing one bandage, she hesitated.

And then he was pulling away.

"The record."

She blinked as if she'd suddenly come from complete darkness into a brilliantly lighted room. "What?"

"The record's over," he said gruffly.

Confused, she stared at his dark expression, trying to decipher what was wrong, and it was a moment before she became aware of the insistent scratching of the needle as it tracked against the record. Her limbs quivering with weakness, she walked into the drawing room, turned the Victrola off, then leaned against the tall mahogany cabinet for support.

She'd never in her life experienced anything like what had just happened between her and Nico. A touch of his lips had sent her out of control—an experience he obviously hadn't shared. *Okay*, she thought, rubbing her forehead, *what now?*

She was torn. She was beginning to wish desperately for something more to develop between her and Nico than a brief brush with passion, although she sensed it would be foolish of her to try to pierce the mystery that surrounded him. But in the final analysis, like the tides and the seasons, some things were inevitable, and she felt she had no choice.

When she came back to the veranda, she found Nico leaning against the balustrade, his shirt buttoned, his arms crossed over his chest. He appeared very hard, very closed.

She halted beside him, facing in the opposite direction, and folded her hands on top of the ornamental barrier. "Did I touch a tender spot?"

"No."

"Were you afraid I would?"

He glanced at her. She was gazing out at the night-shrouded ocean, and the confusion he saw on her face filled him with anger—an anger directed solely at himself. "No."

She ran her tongue over her bottom lip. "I was just wondering. . . . When you were kissing me, you seemed so guarded."

No woman had ever sensed that he was holding part of himself back during any phase of his love-making. He wasn't sure he'd been aware of it himself. Not until now. Caitlin was too perceptive for her own good. "You're mistaken."

"I don't think so."

He ground his teeth together in frustration. Why didn't she just leave it alone? "Maybe I feel it wouldn't be a good idea to become involved with you."

"Is that because you're involved with someone else?" Her heart beat very fast as she waited for his answer, and it seemed a long time coming.

"No."

"Then why, Nico?"

He shot out his arm, clasped the side of her throat, and pulled her in front of him. Each word he spoke carried a biting emphasis. "It could be I'm afraid to lose control with you, because if I did, I wouldn't know where it would end."

She swallowed hard. "Do you really believe that?"

He stared broodingly at her, his thumb stroking up and down the sensitive cord at the side of her neck. "Maybe."

"You're a difficult man to get to know, Nico DiFrenza."

"And you, Caitlin Deverell, are too damn easy to want." Like a junkie needing a fix, he pressed a hard kiss to her lips. It seemed a long time before he released her. But once he did, it seemed too short a time.

He waited for her to say something and cursed the continued silence. This kind of tension couldn't continue. Something had to give between them, or there would be an explosion. "You didn't put on another record."

She folded her shaking hands on top of the balustrade. "No. That's the kind of music I love, but I wasn't sure if you liked it or not."

"When I listen to music, it's usually classical or opera, but I liked what you were playing."

She shifted slightly, so that she could see him better. His answer had been curt, but at least he was talking to her, telling her something about himself. "You don't seem the type of man who would like opera."

The slight upward curve of his mouth surprised her. "Your grandfather raised you with Gershwin and Porter. My great-grandmother raised me with Puccini and Verdi. She's from Italy, and to her, music is opera." His smile slowly faded. "My mother died when I was twelve, but even before then, Elena was a strong force in my life. Now she's ill. Her nurses call me whenever she's having a particularly bad day. It makes her furious when I show up, because she doesn't want me to worry about her. She fusses at me, calling me by my full name, Niccolo, and telling me all the reasons why I shouldn't have come."

An expression of incredible tenderness came over his face, causing Caitlin's breath to catch in her throat.

"I put on *Madame Butterfly* or *La Bohème*, then I sit with her and hold her hand. It never takes long for her to settle down, and soon she begins to talk to me in her native tongue of the times in Italy during the First World War. It was the hardest time in her life, but also the happiest. When she was seventeen, she met and married a young man who was working in the Italian Underground. A year later, he was killed, and she was left widowed and pregnant." He paused. "She goes on and on about those times. Sometimes I wonder if she knows what she's saying. But her mind seems very clear, and somehow talking of those times seems to soothe her."

"I'm sure a lot of it has to do with your being there."

Caitlin's soft voice drew his gaze to her, and he remembered. She was an innocent in all this, a pawn. She had trusted him . . . opened up her home to him. And he was a first-class bastard, a bastard who could easily fall in love with her if he wasn't careful. "We've always been close."

She misinterpreted his flat tone and raised her hand to his face. "I know how you feel. My grandfather's illness was very hard for me to watch. He'd always been such a vital man, but he didn't mind his going as much as I did. He was eager to see Arabella again."

He closed his fingers around her wrist, but he didn't pull her hand away. "His wife?"

She nodded. "I wish I could describe his expression to you—when he drew his last breath."

"You were there?"

"All my life he'd been there for me. I wouldn't have forgiven myself if I hadn't been there for him. And I was glad I was. He seemed so at peace, so happy. I knew without a doubt that he was with Arabella, so I grieved only for myself then."

Why, oh why, did she have to be such a special person? Feeling momentarily defeated, he gave in, drew her into his arms, and just held her.

Caitlin pressed her cheek against his chest. No matter what he'd told her about himself, she was certain there was much, much more to learn. He was a difficult, enigmatic man, but she was beginning to feel just as puzzled about herself. What were these sad-happy, confused-clear feelings she'd been having?

She'd had what she supposed could be termed a few "relationships" over the years, and along the way she had lost the normal number of illusions. She'd learned that fairy tales weren't real and that love could be confusing, sometimes even painful. None of her lessons in love had been traumatic, but now she realized that what she'd experienced in the past was milk toast in comparison to what she was going through with Nico. He shook her to the marrow of her bones.

She lifted her head and brushed a warm soft kiss across his lips. She felt him stiffen, then slowly relax and gather her closer to him. The control was still there, but so was the heat.

And the taste of Nico lingered on her lips long after he'd abruptly and quickly broken off the kiss and gone upstairs to his room. And still she found she couldn't sleep.

In his room, Nico dialed and waited. When the sleepy sound of Amarillo Smith's gravel voice came on the line, he said, "Rill, it's me."

" 'Bout damn time you called. Where are you?"

"SwanSea."

"Good. I was afraid you wouldn't be able to get in."

Nico's mouth firmed. It might have been better if he hadn't. "I'm here. Anything new?"

"Not so far. Just lie low and get well."

It sounded so easy, he thought grimly. "Right."

"Are you in pain, Nico?"

"No."

"I just wondered. Your voice sounded funny there for a minute."

"I'm fine. Have you looked in on Elena?"

"She's doing well."

"Did you check to make sure she has everything she needs?"

"Of course." The acerbic tone of Amarillo's drawl indicated Nico had been stupid even to ask.

Nico's lips quirked. Amarillo had been raised in the oil fields of West Texas, and his frontier mentality made him a law unto himself. No one understood why he was in Boston, but he was as hard and as tough as they came and always got results. And he was the one man Nico trusted with his life.

"Got a pencil, Rill? I'll give you this number."

Three

Ramona, a big-boned woman with shoulder-length salt-and-pepper hair and a no-nonsense manner, filled Caitlin's cup with steaming black coffee, then stood back and fixed her with a critical stare. "Why do have shadows under your eyes? Aren't you feeling well?"

"I feel fine."

"What about those shadows?"

"The sun isn't out today, and the light is probably making every one of us look ghastly." She smiled. "Except you, of course. You always look wonderful."

"So do you . . . usually. And you can quit trying to butter me up."

She sighed. "I'm telling you, the rain is giving the light a gray cast."

"I don't believe a word of it. If you don't start taking care of yourself, young lady, I'm going to have two patients."

"Which you'd love. Come on, admit it. The great sorrow of your life is that you don't have enough people to fuss over."

Ramona's lined face took on a pensive expression. "I always thought Julia would marry and give you brothers and sisters. It would have been the best thing for her."

"I agree." Caitlin's words were sincere, but today she wasn't in the mood to listen to a rehash of what she'd heard time and again. She changed the subject to something she did want to hear. "How's Nico doing? I haven't seen him today."

Since their encounter on the terrace she'd done some serious thinking, and she now realized that Nico was the one who always pulled back when their encounters threatened to become too intimate or, as on the terrace, too passionate. She didn't know why he was reluctant to become involved with her, but she was coming to understand that with all his mystery and passion, he represented a danger to her well-being. And she was no clearer how she felt about him.

Except, she was very much afraid that, in spite of her better judgment, she was falling in love with him. The thing was, she'd inherited the Deverell pride. She'd never in her life pursued a man, and there was no reason why Nico DiFrenza should become the first.

Except she couldn't stop thinking about him. Or aching for him.

"Nico is getting better every day," Ramona said. "By the way, do you know what kind of surgery he had?"

"No." Caitlin smiled ruefully. "In fact, he's never admitted to surgery, just some vague illness. But I'm surprised you haven't asked him."

"Actually, I did. And he told me about his condition. But you know, I don't think he ever answered my question."

"I wouldn't worry about it. Like most men, I think

he's just very sensitive about being ill. Anyway, whatever was wrong with him has obviously been taken
care of."

"I suppose."

Caitlin glanced at her watch. "I better get moving.
Conrad Gilbert is due soon, but before he gets
here, I want to run up to the attic. If I remember
right, there's a chair up there with upholstery I
want duplicated for a suite of rooms in the northwest wing."

Nico rested on his heels and rubbed his neck.
He'd been in the attic for over two hours, and he'd
only managed to search two trunks. He had thought
that over the years, a family like the Deverells would
have devised a more systematic way of storing their
things. Apparently though, they were a family who
tended to move forward, rather than spending time
reflecting on the past. Admirable, but not at all help-
ful to him.

The creak of footsteps on the attic stairway took
him by surprise. Quickly and quietly he shut the lid
of the trunk he'd been searching. By the time Caitlin
entered the musty room, he was standing by an
arched window.

"Nico. I didn't expect to find you up here."

And he sure as hell hadn't expected her to come
up here, he thought, eyeing her warily. She was
wearing a jade-green tank top with a lacy appliqué
on the front and crisscross straps in the back. Her
faded denim shorts had a form-fitting waist and
full, flirty legs that made it resemble a sexy little
skirt. Perfect outfit for mucking about an attic on a
rainy day. Perfect outfit for driving him crazy.

His expression revealed none of what he was feeling but reflected the innocence of a small boy caught in a harmless prank. "It's the rain," he said by way of explanation. "It always makes me want to seek out an attic."

She smiled somewhat nervously as she noted that being away from him for a time hadn't changed the way his presence made her heart race. As startled as she'd been to encounter Nico and despite her recent resolution regarding him, she was very glad to see him. "How long have you had this condition?"

"Since I was a kid. Didn't you tell me you used to like to poke around up here?"

"Yes, and as you can see, I still do."

"Are you poking around for anything in particular?"

"Yes, a chair. I thought I remembered it being in this room, but I'm not sure."

She'd accepted his explanation without question, and he felt as if he were the worst kind of con man. He couldn't leave SwanSea yet, but there was a part of him that half wished she'd throw him out. "Maybe I could help you search for it."

"If you like. It's a pear-wood armchair with curved arms and legs, and cream-and-yellow upholstery."

"I haven't really looked around much, but it could be here. We could each search a different area if you like."

"Okay, but there's no rush." She lifted her tightly linked fingers in an awkward gesture. "What were you doing? I mean, have you been up here long?"

He shrugged. "No, not really. Did you know there's a great view from this window, even with the clouds and rain?"

She weaved her way around trunks, boxes, and an assortment of furniture until she reached Nico's side. "You're right," she said, gazing out the window. "I'd forgotten how much more you can see from up here than down on the bluff."

Driven by a compulsion stronger than his will, Nico studied the pure line of her profile and discovered that her dark lashes feathered against her cheeks when she blinked. *Charming.* And her finely pored skin appeared luminous, even without make-up. *Beautiful.* And her lips parted slightly as she breathed in and out. *Tantalizing.* As he had all day yesterday, he relived the feel of her in his arms.

Without his being able to prevent it, she had gotten under his guard the night before last. He'd told her things about himself and his great-grandmother that no one outside the family knew. The people he could really talk to were so few, he'd been left wanting to tell her more. But that was impossible.

He'd kissed her and hurt to go further. And of course that too was impossible.

On impulse, she unlatched the window and pushed outward on the frame. It didn't budge.

"Stuck?" His voice was slightly husky.

She nodded, trying again. "It hasn't been opened in years."

"Let me see if I can do it." He gave the window one good shove, and it swung outward.

"Thanks. I thought the room could stand a little air." She turned and looked at him, and the smile on her face slowly faded as she took in the intensity of his eyes. She shouldn't read anything into the expression, she told herself. He just happened to be a man with intense eyes.

So he'd kissed her. He wasn't the first.

So she'd melted when she'd never melted before. It meant nothing.

What's inside you, and why do I care so much? she asked him silently. There were layers to this man that no one would discover unless he allowed it—she'd learned that much. And she had resolved that if something developed between them, he would have to make the first move.

But his nearness was sending jittery little thrills skittering along her nerve endings; she stuck her hand out the window and let the gentle rain cool her skin.

Before the cooling was done, he drew her hand in from the rain and brought the inside of her wrist to his mouth. He pressed his lips against the nearly translucent skin and felt her pulse race. Then his tongue darted out to lick away the rain.

"I missed seeing you earlier," he heard himself murmur. What the hell, he thought wearily, he was simply trying to divert her. And licking rain from her wrist was as good a way as any. How could he have known how delectable he would find her flesh?

"I was busy," she said with a catch in her voice.

"That's what Ramona said." He brushed his lips back and forth over the sensitive underskin of her wrist and heard her intake of breath. *Oh, Caitlin, why do you have to be so damned sweet?*

"She told me you were feeling better this morning." He dropped his arm, taking her hand to his side. "As soon as it stops raining, I thought I'd try to jog a little."

Protest sprang immediately to her lips. "You shouldn't. You'll hurt yourself."

"I said a *little*." His dark gaze fixed on her lips, and he bent and placed a kiss at the corner of her mouth. It was as much as he would allow himself. "Don't worry," he whispered, his breath fanning her lips. "I'm very good at taking care of myself." He traced the outline of her lips with his tongue, then again kissed the corner of her mouth. It was enough, he thought. After all, he was just playing. But her shudder tore through him.

"I'm glad."

He'd accomplished what he'd set out to do, he thought. She was distracted. He wouldn't have to kiss her again. He straightened, reached for a lock of her cinnamon hair, and wove it through his fingers. "How about you, Caitlin? Are you good at self-preservation?"

She gave a shaky laugh. "I suppose I'm adequate. I couldn't have reached twenty-six if I wasn't."

"You're just a baby."

Her tongue moistened her bottom lip. "How old are you?"

His gaze followed the action. "Thirty-four." He released her hair and skimmed the pad of a finger across her moistened bottom lip. "But most of the time I feel eighty-four."

Any minute now, she was going to lose track of their conversation, she reflected. All she could think of was how close he was standing to her and how much he seemed to be touching her. "Why would you feel that old?"

"Life, Caitlin," he said roughly. "Life. Take my advice and stay the same age as you are biologically, for as long as you can."

"H—how would you recommend I do that?"

His jaw clenched until he felt pain shoot up the side of his face. "Stay away from me."

"Stay . . ." To her mortification, tears filled her eyes. "What?"

"Damn." He jerked her to him and crushed his mouth to hers. His tongue found the hot velvet of her mouth, and need exploded in him, nearly undo-

ing him. Thoughts crowded into his brain, thoughts of taking her down to the floor with him, undressing both of them, locking their bodies together, and learning her from the inside out. It was a bad, bad idea. It was the wrong time, the wrong place, the wrong person. . . . But Lord, how he wanted her.

Lightly he grated his teeth along the length of her tongue, eliciting a moan from her. Caitlin had no thought of holding back. He'd jerked her to him as if wanting her had gotten the better of him. The idea thrilled her, and at the same time she understood. Maybe there was a reason why she should fight against him and the way he made her feel, but if there was, she couldn't think of it.

He thrust both hands upward beneath the wide legs of her shorts and the lace trim of her panties and took hold of the rounded contours of her bottom. The sensation of kneading the firm flesh satisfied him for only a moment. Everything in him was clamoring for him to bury himself inside her and seek relief for this fever that was driving him crazy. Without relinquishing his hold on her, he lifted her against his pelvis, then pulled her into him hard, so that she could feel the strength of his desire. When Caitlin wrapped her legs around his hips and tightened her hold on him, he nearly came undone.

The fresh smell of rain came through the window and mingled with the scent of their need. They strained together as a dark fire blazed in and around them.

Caitlin felt as if she were balancing on a precipice and the uncertainty made her feel helpless.

Nico had an intense driving need for her, and the certainty made her feel strong.

Uncertainty. Certainty. Helplessness. Strength.

Whatever . . . She couldn't, wouldn't let him go until the hunger growing inside her was assuaged.

The muscles in his back shifted and moved beneath her hands as he began lowering them to the floor.

"*Caitlin.* Caitlin, are you up there?" Ramona called.

Nico stilled and muttered a curse. Then, before she could protest, he set her on her feet and almost ripped her arms from around his neck.

"*Caitlin?*"

"Yes?" she said, but her voice was too weak to reach Ramona who she knew was standing at the bottom of the attic stairs.

"*Caitlin!*"

"Answer her, dammit," he ordered in a harsh whisper.

Nico's eyes were burning with an anger that bore right through her. She cleared her throat and called, "What is it, Ramona?"

"Conrad Gilbert is here."

"Tell him to make himself comfortable, and I'll be down in a few minutes."

"All right." There was a brief silence, then, "Are you okay? You sound—funny."

She bent her head and rubbed her temple. "I'm fine. I'll be down shortly."

The rasping of their heavy breathing sounded loud in the quiet attic room as Ramona's footsteps receded. Caitlin could feel the heat from Nico's body on her skin, but the continued silence between them stretched out until she couldn't take it anymore. Uncaring that her eyes revealed all the hunger she was feeling, she said, "I'll tell Conrad I can't see him today, Nico. I'll— "

"No."

"But—"

His teeth ground together as he reflected how close all his fine resolutions had come to being blown straight to hell. "I said it before, and I'll say it again. Stay away from me."

"What are you talking about? Something just happened between us—"

"Something that damn well shouldn't have." A hard dark mask descended over his face. "Stay away from me, Caitlin, and I'll stay away from you!" He wheeled and stalked from the room.

Caitlin bit her lip and wrapped her arms tightly around her waist. Devastated, she stood very still, knowing it would hurt to move, to think, to recall what had just happened. Long minutes passed, but no relief came.

Finally, slowly, with heavy automatic movements, she began her search for the chair. The sight of the trunk gave her momentary pause. The lock hooked in the hasp wasn't completely closed.

"That's odd," she murmured aloud. "I thought all the trunks were locked."

The next few days blurred for Caitlin. She dealt efficiently with crises as they arose. The morning after the scene in the attic, she discovered that the wrong wallpaper pattern had been put up in one bedroom. Much to the consternation of the workmen, she ordered the paper stripped. The next day, she caught a painter about to use too bold a shade of peach in the main drawing room and had to explain to him that the Art Nouveau period was one of rich but muted colors and that she wanted a softer color. She knew she was being a perfectionist, but where SwanSea was concerned, everything had to be just right.

Obsession with work blocked out thoughts of Nico—sometimes for minutes.

She went out of her way to avoid him, not because he had told her to but because she felt seeing him again would be like exposing an open wound to more injury.

But by the time the electricity blew on the third day, she had begun to be annoyed with herself. Since when had she become so fragile? she asked herself. *Since Nico came to stay,* she answered.

After discovering that a mistake had been made when the new wiring was installed, she put in a call to the electrical subcontractor. Then she realized Nico needed to be told they would be without electricity for a while, perhaps even a few days. Her first thought was to send Ramona to find him, but she quickly vetoed the idea. *Enough of this,* she decided. She had a strong backbone, and it was time she used it.

Nico came to a sudden stop by the marble fountain in the center of the conservatory and lasered a sharp gaze around the immense iron-and-glass building. He heard nothing now, and he knew that he was alone. But . . . just for a moment there, he had thought he heard laughter, like a haunting echo of long ago.

He shook his head, puzzled by the intense interest he felt for the great house, its land, and its buildings. SwanSea was built on the detailed and opulent scale nearly unbelievable and almost impossible to achieve in present times. But his interest went deeper than the awe that was natural upon seeing for the first time the wonders of this century-old house.

But it was as if the house had reached out and taken possession of him, so that slowly he was coming to understand Caitlin and her fierce feelings for her inheritance.

Procrastination had never been a part of his makeup, but this afternoon he had decided to explore more of the grounds of SwanSea instead of continuing his investigation of the attic as he'd promised himself.

He'd taken a stroll over to the pool house, large enough to accommodate a couple of families easily. According to Caitlin, it had been built in the 1920s after her grandfather had taken ownership of SwanSea. Nico had spent some time wandering through its bowling alleys, squash courts, the gymnasium, the Turkish bath, and the fabulous indoor swimming pool. Then he had made his way here.

Sinking onto a wrought-iron bench, Nico exhaled heavily. The sun was setting on the west side of the conservatory. Golden light flowed through the big glass panes, filling the inside of the nearly translucent building with currents of sunshine that coiled and curled around the statues and the orange trees growing beneath the crystalline roof.

His recuperation was coming along nicely, but in a call to Amarillo he had learned it wasn't safe for him to leave SwanSea—too many people were still looking for him. And in a call to his great-grandmother, he had promised her that he would continue his search.

How much longer could he stay here without losing his sanity? He'd had many opportunities over the last few days to watch Caitlin from afar. He'd envied every man at whom she'd smiled. He'd been jealous of anyone with whom she'd spoken. And worst of all, as he lay in bed every night, the knowledge that she was in her room just down the hall chafed at him until he felt raw.

His desire for her had grown daily until he'd almost become used to the pain. That day in the attic had nearly been his undoing. Since then, a lot of his time had been taken up with remembering the way the tantalizing scent of her skin could wind around a man's body until he thought he'd suffocate if he didn't have her.

He had to stay away from her.

"Nico?"

His head jerked around as she made her way along a path between flower beds newly readied for planting. At the sight of her, his body tensed and his chest began to hurt.

Nearing him, she nervously smoothed her damp palms down the full skirt of her sleeveless jade-green sundress. "You're a hard man to track down," she said.

He sensed her unease, but he couldn't smile easily to reassure her, and he couldn't take his eyes off her. Her sudden and unexpected presence had heightened and intensified the aching pain he'd felt these last days—and the sensation was the difference between holding his hands toward a fire and feeling its warmth, and thrusting his arms into the fire.

He came to his feet. "Was there something in particular you wanted to see me about?"

"Yes. We've had some trouble up at the house and—"

"Trouble?" Alarm turned his muscle to steel.

She eyed him warily. "I'm afraid so. We have no electricity." She shrugged, trying for nonchalance. "I'm not sure what happened. Something blew something. The electrician will be out first thing in the morning. Tonight, though, and maybe for a few days to come, it will be candlelight. I thought you should know."

He exhaled slowly. "Thank you. I appreciate your coming to tell me."

"No trouble," she said shortly and laced her fingers together. "I needed to check out what they've done in here anyway, and it looks like they're making real headway. I see they've carted away the debris, replaced the broken panes, and cleaned the windows. They'll probably start on the fountain next." She shrugged awkwardly. "Well, I need to get back. I've got work waiting for me."

An inexplicable panic seized him, and he anxiously searched for something to keep her with him a little longer. "I've never seen anything quite like this building. What exactly is it used for, anyway?"

She was pleased by the genuine interest in his tone. "Originally, it was built to be an indoor garden for people to stroll through, to rest in, to read in—anything, really. But there have been wonderful parties here, and I can guarantee you, there will be again."

His appreciation for the confidence and joy she felt in the great house of SwanSea was newfound. But his pleasure at simply being near her was an ancient, primitive reaction.

There was a tightrope he'd had to walk for many years. Often he'd had difficulties. But he'd never had to remember to keep his balance as he did now. "You plan to rent it out for private functions?"

She nodded. Without her being aware, the subject of SwanSea had given her pale, stiff features a lovely animation. "Yes. And I think it would be perfect for the hotel's regular afternoon tea, with a pianist playing Gershwin and Porter. Or for special dinner parties or events . . . The possibilities are endless."

Her excitement over her plans flushed her skin with luminosity, and Nico decided he'd never seen anyone quite so exquisite and desirable. The sun had been lowering in the sky while they talked, so that the golden light appeared silken and tinted with crimson. To lie down in the light and make love with Caitlin would be the ultimate sensual experience.

"The conservatory has always reminded me of a glass castle," she was saying. "Doesn't it you?"

His mouth twisted with humor. "That wouldn't have been my first thought, no."

Caitlin's gaze went to his mouth, and she was forcibly reminded that her attraction for him was as strong as ever. But unfortunately nothing else had changed either, and the fact that they'd managed to talk companionably for a few minutes didn't alter the fact that she meant nothing to him.

She swallowed against a dry throat. "It looks like some sort of iron and glass fantasy to me. The weblike ironwork appears so delicate, yet it supports all of that glass. Using structural ironwork as part of the decoration of a building was a trademark of Art Nouveau."

Good, he thought—a topic that would take his mind off the desire building inside him. "I guess you're an expert on the period."

"It's part of my heritage, just like DiFrenza's must be part of yours, even though you don't work there."

"I suppose so," he said, unaware that she'd managed to change the focus. "It's true I never developed an affinity for the clothing business, but I did work in the store every summer when I was in school." He grinned slightly. "It made my family happy."

"What sort of jobs did you have?"

"All sorts. I even learned to dress windows."

"Really?"

"Really," he said huskily, "and I also learned fabrics. For instance, I could tell you what your dress is made of." He paused as he realized what he was about to say and do, and then he plunged on. "But I'd have to feel the material."

"All right," she said as a tremor began within her.

Two of his fingers slid beneath the edge of the scooped-out neckline and touched her skin as he grasped the shimmery material of her sundress. The sudden heat from the contact made her gasp.

He heard her and experienced a corresponding quickening. The tactile sensation of her skin and the soft material made him linger, rubbing the material back and forth between his thumb and fingers. He was torturing himself, he thought, but he couldn't stop. "It's a silk linen blend," he murmured.

Caitlin had come to life at his touch. Her pulses were racing, her senses whirling. But no matter what, she knew she couldn't betray what she was feeling. Not this time. She managed to indicate he was right with a slight nod.

With more care than was warranted, he withdrew his hand. "Very pretty."

"Thank you." Her pounding heart sounded in her ears. She moved a few steps away from him and gave the fountain her complete attention. "You know," she said casually, "I don't think you ever told me what type of law practice you have."

He gave a brief prayer of thanks that she hadn't been looking when she asked the question. Otherwise, she would have seen him go rigid. "I'm a criminal lawyer."

She risked a glance over her shoulder. "That must be interesting."

"It's a job."

She contemplated his terse remark, running her hand over the cool marble of the fountain. Nico didn't strike her as the kind of man who would enter a profession about which he didn't care passionately. Otherwise, like his father and sister, he would simply have gone into the family business.

She turned back to him. "But you must enjoy it. You did have other options."

"Not really." He looked away. His fingers still tingled as he remembered the feel of her skin. "Caitlin . . ."

"Yes?"

He gripped his bottom lip with his teeth until all the color had been squeezed from the flesh. Then and only then did he trust himself to speak. "Did Ramona tell you what time supper would be?"

Instinct told her that his inquiry about supper had been an afterthought, but instinct also told her not to probe. He knew as well as she that Ramona would serve him whenever he showed up. "Around seven. Are you hungry?"

He returned his gaze to her, and his throat constricted at the sight she made in the gathering dusk, her cinnamon hair a vivid contrast to the jade-green dress. "Yes," he murmured softly. "Yes." He cleared his throat, taking a moment to get himself together. "I am hungry, but I can wait. I think I'll go back to the house, though, and wash up."

"I have to get back too. I'll walk with you."

They moved at the same time and bumped against each other. The contact was minimal, but the result was magnified by their charged state.

Nico pulled a deep lungful of air into his body, attempting to clear his mind. But the air was filled with sweetness—newly turned earth, orange blossoms, and the knee-weakening fragrance of the woman beside him. Nico closed his hand around her arm and pulled her against him. The taste of her mouth brought a growl from the back of his throat. He deepened the kiss, seeking the warmth and the heat that he had craved every minute of every day since he had last kissed her.

A violent tremor shook Caitlin. The passion of his kiss—the fire skimming along nerve endings, invading the lower part of her body—was heaven, was hell.

She wanted this man, and it would be so easy to give in and surrender to where the kiss would lead. But there were too many things she didn't understand. The memory of his rejection in the attic played like a warped record in the back of her mind.

It wasn't that she didn't have the strength to risk his rejection again. She did. But why should she?

And she could stand the pain she knew love sometimes brought. But only if she had a reason to accept that pain.

Crushed against his body, Caitlin could feel the power of his need for her, yet just days ago he had told her to stay away from him. That meant he didn't *want* to want her.

But his mouth was devouring hers, and his hand was caressing her breast with urgency. She could conclude only that he wanted her in the same way he would want any reasonably attractive woman and that she meant nothing special to him. She had too much pride to allow any man to make love to her when his entire heart, mind, and soul were not involved. Heartsick, she pushed against him.

He felt her hands against his chest, but her resistance was slow to penetrate his raging need. Once his mouth had touched hers, control had vanished, and now his body was set and ready for just one thing—to make her his. He wanted her with a strength that involved every cell of his body.

When he finally realized something was wrong, he could hardly believe it. With an angry sound, he wrenched his mouth away from hers and brought his head up in one movement. His dark brows drew together in a scowl as he concentrated on reassembling the broken pieces of his willpower, and waiting for the pain that held his body in its grip to subside.

"I'm sorry," she murmured. "It's my fault."

"What?" he asked, totally without comprehension.

"You told me to stay away from you. I should have sent someone else to find you. But I thought . . ." She'd thought she would be able to carry on a casual conversation and that if he touched her, she'd be able to hold back all signs of a response. She'd been wrong.

Nico's mind cleared, and suddenly he saw what had happened. He had hurt her badly that day in the attic, but he'd been so caught up with his own agony, he hadn't been able to see it.

Initially, he'd known that just by coming to Swan-Sea, he was taking advantage of her. In his world, right edged toward wrong, but the end always justified the means. He'd intended to get into the house, fulfill his promise to his grandmother, and then get out again without fuss or bother.

But the complications of the situation had been apparent from the start. He wasn't sure if he had been too weak from his wounds to see the complications or if the impact of her green-gold eyes had made him ignore the truth. He also wasn't sure why he now felt such an overwhelming need to protect her. But whatever the reason, he knew what he had to do.

"Caitlin, nothing is your fault."

"But—"

He clasped her shoulder. "No, I mean it. *Nothing* is your fault. You were kind enough to let me stay here when I needed a place to rest and regain my strength. I'm much better now, and I promise you I'll leave as soon as I can make other arrangements."

She couldn't keep the dismay from her voice. "You're going to leave? But, Nico, is it really safe for you to leave so soon?"

Hell no, he thought, but it would be easier to face the type of danger Rettig and his men offered than risk. And he didn't dare risk the danger of hurting her—one more time. He dropped his hand to his side. "I'm better, Caitlin, and I need to leave."

"Very well." Her dignified bearing did not quite disguise the shakiness of her words. "You know what's best for you. When you've made your plans, let me know."

"I will."

"Good. I'll se you back at the house."

Unable to trust himself to speak, he nodded.

And then he was alone in the great iron-and-glass building, the silence and the emptiness engulfing him. Guilt weighed so heavily on him, and he had to sit down.

Sometime later, he heard the sound of someone softly weeping. The sound grew and grew until it rebounded through the conservatory, surrounding him, and he covered his ears.

"Rill? It's Nico."

"Hi. How are things?"

"My recovery is going fine."

"Uh-oh, I hear a *but* coming."

"But I've got to leave here."

Amarillo's voice changed from laconic to tense in a split second. "Rettig?"

"No, no, nothing like that. It's just that . . . Look, if you don't want me to come back to Boston yet, make arrangements for me to stay at another safe place until I can."

"Nico, I thought you were crazy when you told me you were going to try to get into SwanSea, but now that you're there, it's turned out to be perfect."

"I'm glad you're so satisfied with the situation," Nico said, irritation making his words razor-edged.

"I know the waiting is hard—"

"*Hard*, Rill? It's damned impossible."

"Since when has impossible stopped you? And as long as you're in a bad mood, I might as well tell you I faxed photos and rap sheets of Retting and his key people to the local police, just in case we're right."

"Dammit, Rill! I told you from the start I didn't want the local people in on this."

"I saw it differently, so save your breath. It's done."

Nico let out a fluent string of curses that accomplished nothing, not even making him feel better. "Just get back to me with a place, Rill, and don't be too long about it, or I'll strike out on my own."

"You do, and I'll come and kill you myself," Amarillo said, his tone quite pleasant, quite serious.

Four

Caitlin left the study and shut the door behind her with a vicious tug. A few minutes before, she'd glanced out her study window and seen Nico jog by. Against her will, she'd watched him for a time, noticing the natural athleticism that had emerged with his healing. She remembered wondering what he'd be like when he recovered. Now she knew, and she wished she didn't.

She had no idea how long it would take him to make other arrangements, but she knew it was just a matter of time before he left. She had only one question: How long before she forgot how close she'd come to surrendering everything to him? Her mind, her body, her heart.

"What's wrong, honey?" Ramona asked, coming up behind her. "You don't look like you feel well."

Caitlin turned to her. Seeing Nico's white sweater in Ramona's arms, she pressed a finger to her right temple where the pain of her developing headache seemed to be centered. "Where would you like me to start?" she asked wryly.

"That bad, huh?"

"It depends on how you see another twenty-four hours without electricity, and that's an optimistic estimate. To top it off, Rowan's Plumbing has just delivered twenty-five Victorian-style tubs to us."

"Victorian?"

"Boxy with claw feet," she said succinctly. "What makes me so angry is that there was just no excuse for this mistake. I've spoken directly with the company's president several times about my design that called for a tub with flowing, curving lines. He assured me it would be no problem and sent me a refinement of my sketch for approval."

"What are you going to do?"

"I've already called Rowan's. The Victorian tubs will be picked up tomorrow."

"When will our tubs be delivered?"

"Good question, but I'm through worrying about it for today. In the meantime, I'm going to change into a swimsuit, then walk down to the cove. I've got a little headache I'm going to try to swim away."

"That's a good idea." Ramona patted Caitlin's shoulder. "Swimming always makes you feel better. Oh, as long as you're going upstairs, would you mind putting Nico's sweater in his bureau for me? I mended it for him."

Caitlin hesitated. The last thing she wanted was to run into Nico, but she'd just seen him outside, so . . . She took the sweater. "I'll be glad to."

A short time later, Nico wiped his sweat-dampened face with the end of the towel draped around his neck and opened his bedroom door. And he froze.

Caitlin held a 9-mm automatic in her hand, the muzzle pointed toward the ceiling.

Quickly taking in the open bureau drawer and the

sweater lying on the floor, he instantly grasped what had happened.

She stared at him, a look of betrayal on her face. "Why do you have something like this?"

"Put it down, Caitlin. It's loaded."

"I know that. What I don't know is why you brought a loaded weapon into my home."

Holding her gaze, he walked to her, took the gun from her hand, and replaced it in the drawer.

"You didn't unload it," she said.

"No."

"That means either you're expecting trouble or you are the trouble. Which is it, Nico?"

He regarded her cautiously. "You're one tough lady. Many women would have reacted as if they'd found a snake."

"But it wasn't a snake. Answer my question."

Just one more thing that hadn't gone as planned, he reflected wearily. "Sit down."

She didn't move. "Are you about to tell me something I'm going to hate?"

His lips quirked. "I can almost guarantee it."

With hammering heart, she sank onto the end of the bed and drew the tie of her short terry robe tighter around her waist. "Okay. You told me you weren't an ax murderer. I have to say, I'm really hoping you didn't lie about that."

"I'm a cop."

It took a moment for what he had said to sink in. "I thought you were a criminal lawyer."

"A lie of sorts, Caitlin, and a truth of sorts. I do have a law degree, but I've never hung out my shingle. In my job, I practice criminal law every day."

"I see, and are you going to leave it at that, or are you going to flesh out the particulars?"

He saw beneath her calm facade the smoldering

anger. He tugged open another drawer and from beneath a pile of underwear pulled out a black leather case. He flipped it open and handed her his badge. "I'm a detective with the Boston Police Department, Caitlin. For months now, I've been involved in the investigation of a drug lord. I got too close to him."

She smoothed a finger over the badge. "Someone shot you, didn't they? And that's why you were in the hospital. How serious was it?"

He hesitated, choosing his words with care, his habit of playing things close to the vest not easily broken. "It could have been far worse than it was, but it was bad enough."

"Well, that certainly explains a lot." Shaken, she slid off the bed to her feet. "Why didn't you tell me all of this at the beginning?" she asked, her nerves beginning to show.

"Training. That and the fact that I never expected to . . . become involved with you."

She tried a laugh and failed. "*Involved?* Is that what you'd call it?"

Obsession would be closer to the mark, he thought. "I came here because I needed a place to rest and recuperate." *And,* he added silently, *I needed to search your house.* Self-condemnation roughened his voice. "I'm sorry, Caitlin. I never meant to hurt you."

Her chin lifted. "Hurt? No, Nico. Try mad as hell."

"I know this has been a shock."

"Definitely." She turned away from him, her mind in a spin as she attemped to gain some perspective on the matter. So he'd lied to her by omission. What was so terrible? So she was sure there was more he wasn't telling her. Did that give her the right to yell at him and pound her fists against his chest as she wanted to? She turned back to face him. "This person who shot you—did you catch him?"

"That's police business, Caitlin."

She felt as if he'd hit her. "If this person is still out there looking for you, it's *my* business too. You're in my house, and if he comes looking for you—" She saw the odd expression that flitted across his face. "He *is* out there, isn't he? You're still in danger!" Her eyes misted with tears. "Damn you, Nico, you're still in danger!"

"Trust me, Caitlin. You've never been in any jeopardy."

"Trust you?" Her breath caught on a sob; her chest was tight with a strange new kind of pain. She stared at him, realizing he'd completely misunderstood her concern. His gray workout clothes were soaked through with sweat—under his arms, around his waist, and beneath his throat. His black hair lay in disheveled waves on his head. Dampness burnished his olive skin. I hate him, she thought, brushing moisture from her eyes.

"How many times were you shot?" she asked coldly.

"It doesn't matter, Caitlin. They didn't kill me."

"No. But maybe next time . . ."

He shook his head with impatience. "I can't think of things like that."

"Why not? It seems like a sensible thing to be concerned about."

He laughed shortly. "Now you wish I'd turned out to be an ax murderer, right?"

"Not quite." She folded her arms across her breast. "But I am curious as to why someone with a law degree would join the police force."

"Dammit, Caitlin, why can't you just accept what I've told you? I'm not very good at this sort of thing, explaining or talking about myself, I mean."

"Obviously not," she said, sarcasm lacing her tone. "You know, I remember thinking not too long ago that you weren't the kind of man who would enter a profession you didn't care passionately about. I want to know, Nico. Why are you a detective for the Boston Police Department?"

"It's not that uncommon for a lawyer to become a policeman."

"No? I would think it would be more common for a policeman to become a lawyer."

"What does it matter, Caitlin?"

"It doesn't. I said I was curious, that's all."

Damn. Some information about him could be used by his enemies against him and he made it a practice never to reveal the secrets of his soul. But she wasn't his enemy, he reminded himself. He cared about her, and had been able to give her so little. He'd put her through a lot, and truthfully she wasn't asking for much.

Staring at the wall across the room, he tried to find words for something he wasn't sure he'd ever verbalized, even to himself. He started haltingly. "I had a brother. Antonio—Tony. Four years younger. He died when he was nineteen."

Her sympathy was instant. "I'm sorry."

"Yeah, me too. When I was in my first year of law school, he was in his first year of college. He was a great kid, but he was hard on himself. After his death, I learned that he'd always used me as a measure. Unfortunately for him, I was good in school and athletics, and I knew exactly what I wanted to do." He rolled his shoulders as if he carried something heavy there. "For as long as I could remember, I had this burning in me for the law. Looking at me, Tony must have felt rudderless."

"That wasn't your fault."

"No. But I could have paid more attention to what

was going on with him. Maybe if I had, I could have helped him. As it was, he went away to college, and for the first time in his life, he was away from the family, without our support, feeling as if he had no particular ability."

"A lot of kids are like that," she said, wanting to help him.

"Right, but they give themselves time, and eventually they find themselves. Tony was too hard on himself. He didn't see the promise we all saw in him. He put this terrific pressure on himself to succeed, and he got involved with drugs. Within six months, he burned out like a comet. By the time we realized something was wrong and reached out for him, he was gone. He was found dead one morning in his room in the dorm. Cocaine overdose."

His bleak tone tore at her heart. "You weren't to blame, Nico." She put her hand on his arm.

"So I've been told," he said, instinctively flinching away. A touch of comfort to a man walking a tightrope might affect his balance and send him toppling. He couldn't chance the fall. Circumstances beyond his control had set his path, and no matter what, he had to take that path, even though it led away from her.

She withdrew her hand, this rejection added its weight to his other rejections.

"At the time, I felt so damned helpless," he said, continuing on with determination. "I went to the school, looking for a villain, someone I could focus my rage on. What I found enraged me even more. The availability of drugs astounded me, and I discovered that the trails to the people responsible were like a giant cobweb made out of hundreds of tiny easily broken threads. Initially I was looking for a neat ending. Something to make it bearable for me and my family. Instead I found a totally hopeless situation where I could do nothing."

"But you've been trying ever since," she said tonelessly.

"Yes."

"And you'll go on trying," she said, wondering at her sinking heart.

"Yes. I win more than I lose, Caitlin."

It was the idea of him losing at all that bothered her, she realized. Then it hit her. *She loved him.*

Stunned, she took a step back. Despair welled in her heart. *No.* Loving him would be one-sided, hopeless, and agonizingly painful. She couldn't—she wouldn't love him!

She saw him looking at her oddly and realized she must have gone pale. "You're in serious danger, aren't you?" she managed to say. "You were told to leave Boston for your own safety, weren't you."

"I can't talk about that, Caitlin, but there's nothing for you to worry about. I'll be leaving in the morning."

"In the morning," she repeated softly. "In the morning. Right."

"Caitlin—"

"Then just leave," she said, her vision clouding with a red mist, "and the hell with you. I've made a fool of myself over you for the last time, but no more." She began backing out of the room. "No more."

"Fool—wait, what are you talking about?"

"I'm talking about *you*, you self-contained, iron-willed bastard!"

She cut cleanly through the waves, anger, frustration, and heartache making her strokes sharp and powerful. She wanted to forget.

The physical exertion gave her a sensation of freedom. Out here, she was part of a mighty force, and she felt renewed. Here there were no wrong deliveries or paint colors. Here there were no headaches. Here there was no Nico.

Something brushed against her leg. She sliced through the center of a wave, kicking vigorously, reflecting that battling the Atlantic was infinitely easier than loving a man who didn't know how to open up, even when he kissed her passionately and held her as if he had no intention of letting her go.

The water was cool, providing exhilaration, forgetfulness, and peace.

Long fingers snaked around her arm and jerked her around. Fear seized her, and she screamed.

"Caitlin, it's me!"

She couldn't believe her eyes. In her surprise, she inadvertently swallowed a mouthful of water and briefly choked. "Nico, what are you doing?" Kicking to maintain her buoyancy, she glared at him. "What are you *doing* out here?"

"Come back in," he yelled, his face set with a hard dominance. "You're too far out."

Her legs tangled with his as she tried to tread water. She went under and came up sputtering in an explosive mood. "What are you talking about? I'm fine, or at least I was until you came out here. Now you're trying to drown me!" She pushed as hard as she could against him, but his hold on her was like steel.

"Just come back with me, Caitlin. It's too dangerous out here."

"*Dangerous?*" Concentrating on him, she didn't see the wave until she felt it wash over her. She surfaced, coughing and furious. "Dammit, Nico, let me go. I've swum here all my life."

"At least swim closer to the shore."

"No," she shouted. "I won't. I like it out here." Enraged, she gave one hard jerk and freed herself.

An iron band came over her shoulder, crossed diagonally over her breast, and yanked her against him with such force that she lost her breath. "Nico!"

"Just shut up," he said, starting toward shore with her clamped tightly against him.

She fought him, kicking and hitting out, but her blows connected awkwardly.

Nico's lungs burned as they tried to pump sufficient air through his body. When his feet touched the sandy bottom, he dragged her to the water's edge, then collapsed, pulling her down with him to the sand.

"Are you *crazy?*" she demanded, flinging her wet hair behind her shoulder. She saw he was wearing only a pair of briefs. The white knit was plastered to his hard male form, and the ridge of his manhood pressed against the almost transparent briefs. She couldn't tear her eyes away. He resembled a sculpted masterpiece. The water had laid an olive-toned patina of sleek satin over the corded muscles and sinews. A fire rushed through her, momentarily debilitating her. She wrenched her gaze away to see his discarded clothes lying several feet away, next to her towel and robe.

"You were so angry when you left that I came after you," he said, his breathing slowly returning to normal. "Then I saw you swimming out to sea." He took in the heightened color in her cheeks, then his gaze dropped to her breasts mounding perilously above the skimpy top. One good breath, and her nipples would break free, he thought, his stomach clenching, his loins heating.

"Out to *sea?* Lord, how can one man be so stupid? Look at you"—keeping her eyes above his waist, she gestured to the two brilliant red scars across his torso—"you're just out of the hospital, probably not even healed properly yet."

"I'm fine."

"And you scared me half to death out there, coming up behind me like some sea monster, nearly drowning me."

"Me drown *you*? If you hadn't fought me—"

She uttered an exasperated sound and pushed against the sand to get up. He grabbed her. Off balance, she fell against him. The contact sent shock waves through her.

"You're not leaving yet," he muttered.

"Oh, that's really rich," she cried, her eyes alight with an inner fever. Her skin felt uncomfortable, as if it were too tight, too hot, too full of nerves. "I just love the way you give orders. First you tell me to leave you alone. Now you tell me to stay. I'd say make up your mind, Nico, except I don't care anymore."

"Caitlin, listen to me."

"I've listened and listened, but you don't say anything."

"Then maybe we shouldn't talk at all."

He felt as if all control had been stripped away from him, leaving him a primitive man, raw with knife-sharp desire and blazing need.

Adrenalin pumped furiously through her veins. There was something untamed in the way he was looking at her, and at that moment, she'd never felt more alive. Or more frightened.

"Leave me alone, Nico."

"Don't you see, I've tried to do all the right things and ended up doing everything wrong."

"I don't see anything—"

"Then I'll have to show you." With a quick, smooth

motion, he wiped the moisture from her brow, then tangled his fingers in her wet hair.

"Stop, Nico!"

"Sweetheart, if the world came to an end right this moment, I could not stop."

A small cry escaped from her as a hot weakening coursed through her body, shattering all coherent thought.

He reached behind her, and within seconds, the top of her swimsuit fell to the sand. Then she was fighting to pull air into her chest because his gaze was on her breasts and his expression told her he was starving for her. Her nipples were already erect, and her breasts began to throb—for him.

Bending his head, he caught one tip in his mouth and sucked so hungrily and with such raw eroticism that when he pressed her back on the warm sand, she couldn't even think of protesting.

Water quickly dried on their hot flesh. Her swimsuit bottom and his briefs came off. He kneed her thighs apart and came over her. She clutched at his shoulders. The savage expression in his eyes made her realize there would be no leisurely foreplay, nor did she want it. She was frantic for his possession.

He braced himself on his elbows and gazed down at her, the skin of his face drawn taut with powerful male lust.

"Caitlin," he said, as though her name had been dredged up in an agony of wanting from his gut. Then he surged into her—so easily, so naturally, it was as if it were meant to be.

Filled completely with him, she held his gaze, unable to look away or close her eyes. This moment was too electric for less than all her senses. She wanted to see the changing expressions on his face as he moved in her. She wanted to hear his rough sounds as he felt her tighten around him. She wanted to feel the way his muscles bunched as the ecstacy grew. She wanted to know the taste of his mouth as he thrust into her time after time with a passionate violence.

He showed her no mercy, but he also showed her no control.

The sun, the wind, the surging ocean, and Nico—unyielding elements that couldn't be fought, not now at any rate. No matter how she might wish it were different, she loved him.

He thrust again, and red-hot pleasure flooded through her. She cried out and arched up to him, taking him deeper into her.

The ocean sent its waves spilling to the shore, its lacy foam curling around their feet. He wrapped her legs around his waist, binding her to him in a wild primitive rhythm, and they crested together, hard and intense, their cries mingling and filling the deserted cove.

Time passed, waves rolled into the shore, a bird glided out to sea on a current of air. Finally, Nico rolled to her side but kept his arm around her.

Only then did she close her eyes and lay motionless, willing her body and mind back to normal. It took awhile, but her breathing evened and her senses steadied. Passion died; anger and hurt returned.

She could call herself stupid all day long, she told herself wearily, and it wouldn't change the fact that they had made love. Besides it had been inevitable. But now their storm of desire had passed, and she had to deal with its aftermath.

With the warmth of his body against her, she was tempted to turn her head, bury her face against his chest, and spill her heart and soul to him. She resisted.

Nico might be holding her to him at this moment, but at any minute, he would push her away. It was his pattern. And if his rejection had hurt before, what kind of pain would she have now after experiencing his lovemaking that had left no part of her untouched?

She drew free of his arm, got to her feet, retrieved her swimsuit, and quickly slipped on both pieces.

"Caitlin?" He raised up on his elbow and frowned. "What are you doing?"

"I don't see what difference it makes," she said, bending to scoop up her robe and shrug into it, "but if you must know, I'm going back to the house."

He wasn't sure what he'd expected, but it was definitely not this cold, indifferent attitude. "I don't understand."

"Then let me explain. In spite of your attempts ever since you've been here not to get too intimate with me, we've just made love—if you'll excuse the euphemism. I'm sure you're embarrassed and sorry about the whole thing, but don't be." She picked up her towel and neatly folded it. "You were already planning to leave in the morning. To my way of thinking, you couldn't ask for a neater, less complicated ending than that."

"Caitlin—"

"I've got to go now. I'm sure we'll see each other again before you leave, perhaps at dinner."

Nico sat up and braced his arms on his upraised knees. He stared out at the sea, not trusting himself to watch Caitlin as she climbed the steps to the top of the bluff. He wanted with everything that was in him to run after her, stop her, and bring her back. His body throbbed mercilessly to have her again. And his heart felt as if it were breaking apart.

To stop himself from going after her, he made

himself think of Rettig and a long-buried secret—
two things that could hurt her if he stayed.

Two six-branched silver candelabra sat at either
end of the walnut kitchen table, their candles sending a white-gold pool of light over Caitlin, Nico, and
Ramona. Six other candelabra stood on the sideboard behind them, their candles ready to be lit.
Caitlin stared at her empty plate, trying to recall
what she'd just eaten. She supposed it was possible
that for once in her life, Ramona had slipped up and
given her an empty plate for dinner. Possible, but
not likely.

I am not going to lose it, she thought fiercely. She
put down her fork and reached for her water glass.
All she had to do was concentrate on tomorrow when
Nico would be gone. After he left, she'd be fine.

Peering over the edge of the crystal rim, she studied him from beneath her lashes. He'd been quiet
during dinner, speaking only to answer Ramona or
to compliment her cooking.

"I think I'll drive down to Boston next week," Ramona was saying. "There are a few things I should
check on at home, and—"

"Home?" Nico interrupted unexpectedly.

"I live with Julia, Caitlin's mother," Ramona said.
"She has a home in Boston, and, as a matter of fact,
so does Caitlin." She turned to Caitlin. "I'll run by
your place too, honey."

"There's no need. The security firm's watching it
for me."

"I know, but it's no bother, and I'll feel better."

Caitlin smiled at her. "Thank you."

"You're welcome. And now that I've met you, Nico,
I think I'm also going to do a little shopping at

DiFrenza's. I've been in there a time or two with Julia, but I've never—"

"You mean Caitlin is going to be left all alone in this big house?" Nico asked, interrupting again, this time in a more strident tone.

Both women looked at him, startled. "I've stayed here by myself before," Caitlin said. "When I was in college, I'd sometimes drive up to get away from everything so that I could concentrate on studying."

"And there is Ben Stephenson, you know," Ramona said. "He's always around."

"That's not exactly reassuring," Nico said grimly.

Caitlin blinked, uncertain why Ben Stephenson would bother him. "Why not?"

"The man has been around forever. I ran into him on one of my walks around the estate, and we talked. He's very nice, but the fact is, he's an elderly man, overdue for retirement. I don't know how he's managed to look after this place all alone for as many years as he has."

"He's had help," Caitlin said defensively. "We've always paid a special fee, so the county sheriff's department would keep an eye on things for us. On those occasions when vandals have threatened, we've hired off-duty sheriffs for security until the problem's passed. The main thing Mr. Stephenson has done for us over the years is keep us alerted to trouble."

"That's all well and good, but how can he alert anyone to trouble when he's out in his cottage and you're up here alone?"

"I'll be fine," she said quietly. *Heartbroken and lonely*, she thought, *but fine.*

"She really will be, Nico," Ramona said. "Now *I'd* be afraid to stay here by myself. I'd never get a minute's sleep. There are just too many empty rooms, strange shadows, and unexplained noises for my taste. But Caitlin is a child of SwanSea. She knows this house, and this house knows her."

"It's not the house that bothers me," he said, staring broodingly at Caitlin.

"I wouldn't leave her here alone if I wasn't sure she'd be all right," Ramona said in a tone that made it clear she felt she had brought the subject to an end. "Now, would you like some more wine?"

He shook his head and pushed back from the table. "I think I'll explore the library for a while and see if I can find a book to read."

"By candlelight?" Caitlin asked in surprise.

"Sure. Why not?" Anything to try to get his mind off her and his leaving her in the morning.

Ramona waved her hand toward the candelabra lined up on the sideboard. "Take a couple of those with you."

"One will be fine." He cast a glance at Caitlin. Her head bent, she was studying the crystal goblet in front of her. What was she thinking about, he wondered bleakly. Had he made her hate him?

He shifted slightly. A current of air waved outward from his body, and the candles flickered, sending ripples of white-gold light through the cinnamon strands of her hair. But Caitlin didn't move.

"Good night," he said.

Five

Caitlin's shadow was her only companion as she paced the length of her candlelit bedroom. Sleep eluded her. Thoughts of Nico filled her mind. Initially, he had attracted and intrigued her. Then he had evoked sympathy, desire, and full-blown passion. And finally he had made her fall in love with him.

Remembering those times she'd had an uneasy feeling about him, she paused by a table crafted in an exquisite marquetry floral design set in front of drawn silk-embroidered drapes. The silver candelabrum she had placed there that resembled a six-bud rose tree held tall cream candles. She had been surrounded by beauty like this all her life and assumed that Nico, being a DiFrenza, had too.

He'd spoken of his great-grandmother, told her that he was a police detective and why, but there was still so much she didn't know about him.

She knew what had happened between them from her point of view—she had fallen deeply in love with him, in love with the vulnerable and passionate man she'd sensed beneath the enigmatic surface.

But if he left in the morning without her trying to

talk to him one more time, she would never have a chance to find out what had happened between them from his point of view. She stiffened with indignation. Maybe he would never return her love, and maybe she'd never see him again, but she'd be damned if she would go through her life wondering why he hadn't been able to love her.

Intent on setting out to find him, she turned sharply and struck her hip against the side of the table, sending the candelabrum tumbling.

Nico stood outside Caitlin's door, his hand raised to knock. It seemed as if he'd been frozen in that position for an eternity, his reason warring with his feelings. But peace of mind refused to come regarding what would happen if he knocked on the door and she refused to answer. Slowly, he lowered his hand.

Seeing Caitlin now wouldn't be fair. He had absolutely nothing to offer her, nothing other than a raw, aching need that wouldn't let him alone. Nothing more than a love that because of the less than honorable circumstances under which he was in her house, he didn't feel free to confess.

She deserved honesty and one hundred percent of him, and right now, he couldn't give her either.

He stuffed his hands in his pockets, and with shoulders hunched, turned to go. Then he heard her cry out.

He opened the door, rushed in, and in that moment learned the true meaning of fear. Flames were steadily eating their way up the length of one set of draperies and onto another. To his horrified eyes, Caitlin appeared completely defenseless in her bare feet and skimpy pink-satin chemise, trying to fight the angry red fire with only the coverlet from her bed.

Intent on battling the flames, she didn't realize Nico had entered the room until he lifted her and carried her to safety by the doorway.

She struggled against him. "The fire, Nico. I've got to put it out."

"*I'll* take care of it. *You* call the fire department."

She tried to push past him. "By the time anyone gets here, the whole house will be cinders."

He took a grip on her arms to hold her still. "Then, dammit, do exactly as I say. Stay right here, and I'll put it out."

"But—"

"You're wasting a hell of a lot of time, Caitlin."

Immediately she took a step back and held up her hands. "Do it. For heaven's sake, just do it."

The sob in her voice spurred him to action. He ripped the drapes down and hurled the coverlet over both sets. He made a few stomps over the mound, then dragged the blanket off the bed and jerked more draperies from the walls, throwing all of them on the pile. Gradually the fire was suffocated until there were only smoke and the acrid smell of burnt textiles.

"Are you all right?" Caitlin asked at his side.

"I thought I told you to stay over there."

"Let me see your hands. Oh Lord, you've burned them."

"No, they're just dirty."

"Let's run cool water over them to clean them, and then we'll be able to tell." Shock and the trembling that came with it had started to set in, but tending to his wounds was uppermost in her mind.

"In a minute. First, I want to open these windows and get this smell out of here, then make sure the carpet's not smoldering somewhere that we haven't seen yet." Soon a fresh ocean breeze was blowing through the room. He kicked the burned pile of curtains out to the balcony and inspected the carpet. Finally, he was satisfied, and he gave Caitlin his full attention.

Her eyes were wide as she watched his every move. "You shouldn't have put yourself in danger like that," she murmured.

"*Me?*" He had a great urge to shake her for putting *herself* in such terrible danger. "Look at yourself. You're nearly naked, and you were trying to put the fire out with your hands."

"I had the coverlet."

He wanted to take her in his arms, hold her tightly against him, and let her sweetness flow into him so that he'd forget the sight of the fire rising behind her like some menacing monster. He settled for returning to her side and venting his frustration. "Lord, Caitlin, what if I hadn't been passing by? What if you'd fallen and hit your head and been knocked unconscious? You could have died of smoke inhalation, maybe even burned to death."

He must care, she thought absently. She was still somewhat numbed by the near disaster, but he must care at least a little about her. But was *caring a little* enough for her? "None of those things happened."

"No. Not this time, but this is exactly why you shouldn't stay here by yourself next week."

"Then stay with me," she said abruptly.

Her quiet request was like a sudden punch in the stomach. He closed his eyes and shook his head. "I can't, Caitlin."

"Why?"

When he looked at her again and saw the shock

that lingered in her eyes, he groaned. "Lord, what am I thinking of?" He swept her up in his arms and strode out of the room. "You need to be wrapped up and put in bed."

"I don't have any more bedrooms made up."

His arms tightened. "That's all right. You're staying in my room tonight."

Nico's bedroom was quiet; all its sharp corners and edges were softened by shadows. Candles rising from a tall silver candelabrum emitted a pale glow that spread over the bed's cream-satin coverlet and lapped at the surrounding circle of dark.

He still cradled her in his arms, and to Caitlin, there was something infinitely right about the way her body fit against him, as if in some far distant past, they had been made from the same piece, separated, and were now together again. It was the same feeling she'd had this afternoon when he'd thrust into her.

"Why did you bring me here?" she asked in the hush.

He felt her warm breath against his cheek. Without choice, his hold on her tightened. "You've had a shock. I think the best thing for you would be to get into bed and cover up."

She considered that. "And you? Where will you be?"

"Downstairs, somewhere, on a couch."

They had had hot passionate sex on the beach, but she had never spent the night in his arms, and now it appeared she never would. The idea was strangely unacceptable.

But she had to accept. She *had* to.

Her gaze dropped to his jaw and the muscle that

briefly flickered, then returned to his taut profile.
"At least let me see to your hand."

Slowly he eased his hold on her and let her feet
slide to the floor until she stood without his support. His arms felt curiously empty. The pink-satin
chemise followed her body's shape, skimming over
her breasts, catching on the tiny outward jut of her
nipples, making a slight indentation at her waist
before caressing the rounded curves of her hips and
ending at her thighs. "You're going to get chilled,"
he said, his voice husky.

"Being chilled is not my problem."

Her whispered response went straight through him
like a scorching wind that left him parched for the
taste of her. And when he looked into her eyes, he
saw the shimmering reflection of a candle's flame.
Almost desperately, he reached for the fast-fading
remnants of his strength. "I'm only trying to take
care of you, Caitlin."

"I know that, but why?"

Out of thin air, he created a reason. "Because you
took me in when I needed a place to stay."

"Oh. So you're grateful to me?"

Caitlin in this mood was as dangerous as any gun
he'd ever faced, and his tone was wary. "That's right."

"Then since you're so grateful, give me something
I need."

"What?"

"Help me understand you."

A sardonic smile lifted a corner of his mouth.
"Trust me. Understanding me wouldn't help a thing."

"I think it would."

She was tenacious, and he could tell that she wasn't
going to give up easily. He felt assaulted by her questions and her sensuality, and he badly needed a reprieve
from her. In her bare feet, wearing a scrap of nothing,

her hair tousled in silky waves around her face, she looked too soft, too sweet, too sexy. In short, too damn much like everything he'd ever wanted.

And though he no longer held her, he could feel the heat coming from her body in waves, battering him, bruising him with need.

"You're right," he muttered. "I should do something about my hands."

He disappeared into the darkness of the bathroom, and she heard him turn on the tap. Staring after him, she tried to recall the moment after the fire when the idea had occurred to her that he might care. She wondered if she'd been right. Obviously he had been concerned for her safety. But was it only the concern one would feel for someone owed a favor? At this moment, she didn't have a clue. Only a newfound hope. She might be setting herself up for another fall, but it did seem that he had held her longer than necessary once they'd reached this room.

"Let me see your hands," she said when he returned.

"They're fine."

"Then you won't mind if I check them, will you?" she asked mildly, taking his arm and leading him to the candelabrum. In the brightness, she smoothed her hand across his, straightening his fingers to look for any sign of burn.

Her touch was as light as the brush of a butterfly's wing, its effect nearly catastrophic.

Tentatively she pressed a finger against the hard flesh of his palm. "Does that hurt?"

He swallowed hard. *Not as much as having you this close to me.* "No."

She gave the other hand the same thorough inspection. When she finished, she kept the hand in hers. Lightly, idly, she rubbed the tops of his knuckles. "You were lucky. You could have been burned."

"So could you." Compulsively, he stroked his free hand down her spine.

The warmth from the candles caressed the side of her face. The warmth from his hand gliding down her back curled and gathered and grew, deep inside her. "No, not really."

"Yes, dammit, really. I've never seen anything like it. You think more of this house than you do of yourself."

"You're exaggerating."

"Sweetheart, those flames were no exaggeration." He reached out and stroked a finger across her cheek. "When I think of what those flames could have done to this skin—" The horror of his thoughts was apparent in the shakiness of his voice.

"It sounds like you really care."

He took his hand away. Their lovemaking this afternoon was a living, vivid memory. His body clamored to have her again. It would be so easy . . . so wonderful . . . so mindbending. And that was the trouble. He couldn't let his mind be rearranged. He would only hurt her more than he already had. Just now, he'd made a grave mistake by allowing his emotions to get the better of him. Now he had to try to repair the damage. "Of course I do," he said in a casual, offhand way.

"How much, Nico? How much do you care?"

His dark brows drew together with annoyance, at himself and the circumstances that wouldn't allow him to be honest with her. "What kind of question is that?"

"A legitimate one. You see, you confuse me."

"There's nothing to be confused about," he said impatiently.

His sharp reply didn't disturb her. She sensed she was close to the answers she so desperately needed.

"Really? Then make me understand how you can kiss me one minute and tell me to leave you alone the next. And how you can make love to me on the beach in the afternoon, then tell me that you'll be leaving the next morning."

Yes, Nico, why don't you do that? He felt the tightrope give a wide swing beneath him, and he reached for brutal honesty to keep him steady. "I kissed you and made love to you because I wanted to, more than I wanted to draw my next breath. I'm leaving because it's best for you."

"That sounds like you think you might hurt me."

"Caitlin . . ."

"Do you think you'll hurt me?"

He could feel something breaking apart in him, but he continued to fight. With Caitlin, he needed honor, and he had a short supply. He slid his hand along the side of her neck and with a thumb beneath her chin, tilted her face up to his so that she wouldn't miss one word of what he was about to say. "If I don't leave in the next minute, I can almost guarantee that I will."

She studied his stern, closed expression. There was so much she didn't know about him, so much she might never learn. But it was plain she had two choices: accept him as he was, or back away. The struggle on his face and the warning he had given her told her that in his way, he was trying to play fair. Or as much as he could, considering all that had already gone on between them. "You told me yourself that I'm tough. Remember?"

"Yes, but I don't want to put you in the position of having to find out how tough you are."

"Perhaps, Nico, you already have."

It seemed to him at that moment that her eyes

could see all the way to his soul. His teeth ground together as the pressure built inside him. "Maybe."

"You can be sure of it."

"No. I'm not sure about anything anymore. Except, Caitlin, that wanting you is eating me up inside."

"Inside?" With a boldness she wouldn't have had this morning, she pushed his sweater up until she could run her palm over his abdomen. "Inside here?"

He couldn't control the shudder of hunger that ripped through him or his reply. "Yes. And lower."

Holding his gaze, she unbuckled his belt and undid his pants. His hand shot out to close over hers in a painful grip. Agony registered on his face and in the rawness in his voice, as if it hurt him to speak, to breathe. "I want you to know, if you go any further, you won't have a choice. Despite all my sins and despite all my crimes, you will be mine."

"Sins, crimes, whatever—my choices are all gone, Nico."

With a harsh, fragmented sound, he yanked her against him and brought his mouth down on hers with an urgent, demanding need. She was right, he thought hazily. Choices had disappeared long ago.

Her arms wrapped around his neck and held him tightly. Someone was trembling; she was sure it was she. But when she arched her back to press her breasts against his chest, a tremor racked his powerful body, and she knew she wasn't alone in this wild, magnificent madness.

Control lost once could be rationalized away. Control lost twice had to be accepted. In the past, control had meant the difference between life and death. Now all his protection was peeling away, leaving him forever defenseless to this woman he held in his arms. He was left with nothing but a fierce passion and an undying love for her.

He backed her against the bed, then lowered her to the cream-satin coverlet and followed her down, entering a world of soft hues, sensual textures, and blazing passions.

The chemise had ridden up, revealing narrow pink panties and ivory skin. With a groan, he pressed his face into the softness of her belly.

Hot sweetness flooded through her. She inhaled sharply and held her breath, waiting for what was to come next, the expectancy a pleasure all its own. Then his tongue darted out to lick at her, and a low, broken moan escaped from her throat.

The honeyed taste and satiny feel of her against the roughness of his tongue was a revelation to him. But the tiny shivers that coursed just beneath her skin brought him special delight. Gently he bit his way across her smooth flat stomach. Not a single mark showed his path—only a trail of fire.

He eased her panties down her legs and off her feet. The picture she made, her hair spread out around her, intensified every emotion he was feeling. She was alluring colors, shapes, and textures. She was woman—his woman—with long lovely legs and the cinnamon triangle of hair at the apex of her thighs. "I need to see all of you," he said, his voice a hoarse, desperate whisper, his endurance almost at an end.

"Yes." She lifted the pink-satin chemise over her head, then lay back.

The sight of her struck awe into his soul. The golden hue of her skin had never been more distinctive than it was against the cream coverlet. Her luminosity was almost blinding.

He stripped off his sweater and bent to brush his

lips against the hair between her legs. Involuntarily, her muscles contracted and her hips moved, giving him a deep satisfaction and reminding him that the most sensitive, most secret part of her awaited. His hand began to stroke her gently while his mouth fastened on the taut peak of her breast. His hunger for her was almost excruciating, but he was intent on making this the most pleasurable experience of her life, and he set about using all his efforts to that purpose.

She gripped his shoulders as a shudder of rapture tore through her. His every caress and kiss sent wildfire through her veins. He lathed her nipple with his tongue, and she felt as if she was going to spiral away.

Suddenly, urgently, Nico shifted and rose over her. "There's so much I want to do to you and with you," he said, his breathing rapid and uneven.

"Show me."

Caught in a savage tension, he gave a rough laugh. "We're going to need all night."

"We have that, and more."

"Not now. *Now* I've run out of time. . . ." He quickly undressed, moved over and into her. She was ready, but he wasn't. He'd thought he'd known passion before, but he'd been wrong. Once completely sheathed inside her sweet tightness, a wall of fire crashed over him, debilitating him, sucking all strength and air from his body, leaving nothing but a pulsing, merciless need, and he had to pause to catch his breath. For a moment, he was helpless against the incredible onslaught of feelings. Was it remotely possible that it could always be like this? he wondered. The thought was almost impossible to believe. But his answer came when she began to undulate and strain against him. A driving force took possession of him, and he knew that it would be.

A floodgate opened, sending unbelievable pleasure in cascades over them, drenching them with ecstasy until they were saturated and could take no more.

The candles burned lower and lower, their flames dancing unnoticed in the heated air. And there was no relief from the rapture. It continued through the night.

Gradually, one by one, the candles guttered down and went out. Finally, at dawn's first light, Nico and Caitlin fell asleep, tangled together, arms and legs, hearts and minds, bodies and souls.

Caitlin's hair spilled over one bare shoulder in a shining fall as she came up on her elbow and gazed down on Nico's sleeping face. The wariness had come back over him while he slept, but she wasn't concerned. Last night they had shared something extraordinary, and all her doubts and confusion had vanished.

Through his lovemaking, she'd learned that he was a giving, generous, caring person. She'd learned that he could be both gentle and strong, tender and erotically rough. And if when he opened his eyes this morning and looked at her, she saw an expression that was difficult to read, she wouldn't worry. She'd learned he cared for her, and she believed with all her heart that love could grow from caring.

Adoringly, her gaze strayed over him, stopping to study the leanly muscled torso and the broad chest covered with a mat of curly black hair. At times in the night she had lain limply on his chest, fighting for breath and covered in sweat. He had soothed her, murmuring reassurance. And then they had started again.

A brief frown creased her forehead as she noticed the two angry red scars—aberrant marks against the perfection of his sleek, dark skin. The position of his body prevented her from seeing the entire length of the wounds, but she remembered their ridged feel beneath her fingertips. When she thought of the damage the bullets had done to his body, she gave thanks that he had escaped with only scars.

She reached out a hand to smooth a dark lock from his brow. His long thick lashes lifted to reveal warm smiling brown eyes.

"Did I wake you?" she asked.

"Yes. Did you intend to?"

She grinned. "Yes. I decided as long as I was awake, you should be awake too."

"That's what you decided, was it?"

She nodded, enjoying his morning voice. It had the relaxed, husky timbre of intimacy. "It's nice watching you. You wake gently, as if you're saving your strength for what will come next."

"What do you think will come next?"

A sudden erotic urge flashed through her. "Something wonderful," she murmured, and was taken completely by surprise as he shifted his position, cupped one of her breasts with his long fingers, and drew the nipple into his mouth. Her head went back, and her eyelids fluttered closed as an all-consuming heat took possession of her. He tugged and teased at the tormented point until she gasped and cried out. Then he pulled her mouth down to his and kissed her long and deep.

"Good morning," he said when he was done.

She slid down beside him, facing him, and threw her leg over his hip. She didn't know what time it was, and she didn't care. Activity had probably begun in other parts of the house, and decisions were waiting to be made. But she didn't care about that either. He controlled her. And if he wanted, she'd stay in this bed forever. "Promise me we can always wake up together like this."

A low growl came from his throat. He pushed her over onto her back and surged powerfully and deeply into her, his muscles now coiled, his expression savage with desire. "If I have anything to say about it, we will."

She choked back a cry, wrapped herself around him, and let the wildness begin.

A long time later, the harsh, insistent sound of knocking and a faraway voice pierced through the softness of her dreams. She felt the mattress shift with Nico's weight as he sat up. Rubbing her eyes clear of sleep, she saw that he was pulling on a pair of pants. "Who is it?"

"Ramona. You stay put. You don't want to shock her." He pressed a quick kiss to her mouth, and without taking the time to fasten his pants, he got up and crossed the room. He opened the door only a few inches, angling it so that the view of the bed was shielded.

"Nico, I'm sorry to bother you, but I'm trying to find Caitlin."

Swiftly he tossed various options around in his head, but found none he liked. How in hell could he ease Ramona's mind while protecting the reputation of the woman in his bed? "Caitlin?" he repeated.

"I think I told you that she never eats breakfast, but she usually checks in with me sometime during the morning. When she didn't, I went looking for her. Mr. Haines hasn't seen her, and neither have any of the men. Then I checked her bedroom. Nico, there was a *fire* in there."

He sighed and rubbed the bridge of his nose. The fire couldn't be explained away. "Yes, I know."

"You *know*?"

"I helped her put it out."

"Was she hurt? Where in the world is she?"

"I'm right here, Ramona." Caitlin pulled the door from Nico's grasp and swung it open. "And no, I wasn't hurt."

Ramona's eyes widened as she took in Caitlin, wrapped in nothing but a sheet and standing next to a half-dressed Nico.

"I knocked a candelabrum over in my room last night, and the candles caught the drapes on fire. Luckily, Nico was passing by, and he put it out. Then, of course, I needed a place to sleep."

"Of course," Ramona said.

"We're sorry if we shocked you," Nico told her.

"You didn't shock me," Ramona said gruffly. "I was just worried about Caitlin, that's all."

"Well, I'm sorry I worried you. I should have let you know where I was, but . . ." She cast a helpless glance at Nico, who merely grinned back at her.

"Never mind," Ramona said, back to her brisk, no-nonsense self. "Now that I know you're all right, I'll get started cleaning up your room."

"Those drapes are heavy," Nico said. "Just leave them, and I'll take care of them."

"Never mind. One of the men will help me. In the meantime, I'll air out another bedroom. I don't think you'll want to sleep in there until the smoke damage has been seen to, do you, Caitlin?"

"No. You're absolutely right."

Ramona nodded and looked at Nico. "Can I assume you won't be leaving this morning?"

"Uh, yes, I won't be leaving this morning."

"Fine. Caitlin, later, when you get ready to move your things, you come and get me if you want help."

"I'll do that," Caitlin said.

Ramona turned on her heel and strode off. Nico shut the door. For perhaps thirty seconds, he and Caitlin stared at each other, then burst out laughing.

"Poor Ramona," he said.

"She'll be all right. She's seen a lot in her life. I'm sure she was more embarrassed than shocked."

"I think I just fell off her list of people she likes," he said, steering her against the door and at the same time, unzipping his pants.

Caitlin's sheet slipped unnoticed to the floor as she wrapped her arms around his neck and gazed lovingly up at him. "Not at all. You wait. Next time she sees you, she'll be back to normal. In fact, I'm sure she plans to ignore the whole thing, as if it never happened."

"And she's going to prepare another room for you and move all of your things in, so that at night she can think of you in there rather than in here with me."

Caitlin nodded. "You got it."

He pushed his pants down, out of the way. Then with his hands cupping her bare buttocks, he lifted her, sliding her spine up the door until their eyes were level. "But you *will* be in here with me, won't you?"

She circled his body with her legs and threaded her fingers up into his hair. "Unless you kick me out."

"Me?" he said and pushed high into her. "Lord, you've gotta be kidding."

• • •

Later that afternoon, Caitlin descended the grand staircase, with Nico beside her.

"I'm no expert, but I'm willing to bet this embroidery is going to be expensive to reproduce," Nico was saying regarding the piece of undamaged drapery they had salvaged from Caitlin's bedroom.

Caitlin's happiness was so pervasive, even the damage didn't trouble her. They made the turn on the landing in front of the Tiffany window and started down the last flight of stairs. "I'll shop around. I don't want to have to settle for the *feeling* of the original. If at all possible, I want it to be exactly the same as the original."

"You know, Caitlin," he said, humor threading his voice, "most people involved with restorations are content to use fabrics and furnishings that are of the *type* of the period."

"But this is SwanSea."

Nico smiled wryly. "Right. How could I have forgotten?"

Caitlin laughed. "I admit it. I'm obsessive."

"Be obsessive about me, and I won't mind a bit." One minute he was smiling down at her; the next, he had tensed. "Looks like you have a visitor," he said, indicating the silver-haired man standing just inside the front doors. "Is he the electrical inspector you were waiting for?"

"Could be. I guess I'd better go check."

"I think I'll come with you to meet him if you don't mind."

"Of course I don't."

As she crossed the wide stretch of marble toward the newcomer, Caitlin studied him. An older man, he was fashionably dressed in taupe-colored linen slacks, an open-necked blue shirt, and a navy sport coat. Tall and well built, he had hazel eyes and an attractive, slightly weathered face that made it impossible to guess his exact age. She supposed he was one of those fortunate men who seemed to stop aging in their forties and then began again sometime in their sixties. Nico would probably be one of those men, she thought idly.

As she drew near, she realized with amusement that he was studying her as closely as she had been studying him. "I'm Caitlin Deverell, and this is Nico DiFrenza. May I help you?"

"I'm Quinn O'Neill," he said, nodding to Nico and extending his hand to her, "and I'm delighted to meet you."

"How do you do," she said, shaking his hand. "I assume you're the electrical inspector?"

Humor flashed in his eyes. "No, no, I'm afraid not. I'm just a long-time admirer of the house. I'm on holiday in the area, and I thought I'd take the opportunity to stop by."

He spoke without an accent, yet used a European-flavored phrase. Caitlin decided he must have lived overseas for a time. "I'm sorry, Mr. O'Neill, but SwanSea isn't open yet."

He nodded, his expression intent. "I can see that you're in the middle of work. When do you plan to open?"

"Next spring."

"So long?"

His tone carried a hint of wistfulness, and his manner conveyed a warmth that Caitlin responded to.

He grinned. "You'll have to forgive me. I'm really disappointed. I had hoped I could stay here for a few days."

Caitlin was tempted to laugh. Two men with the same wish in such a short time. Apparently she was going to have no trouble booking guests. "You wouldn't want to stay here now, believe me. Things are a real mess. We don't even have electricity at the moment."

"I really wouldn't mind. You see, I stayed here once a long time ago."

Caitlin's interest sharpened. "Really? When?"

"I can't remember exactly . . . as I said, it was many years ago. But I've always remembered SwanSea as a very special place."

"Were you here visiting my grandfather?"

Quinn nodded. "Jake was a wonderful man. I was sorry to hear of his death."

"Thank you."

Standing beside Caitlin, Nico realized his shoulders were tensed and his instincts were telling him to be wary. He'd felt this way before in the presence of dangerous men. But he had to wonder, could he trust his instincts in this situation? Or was he simply experiencing the prickly awareness one male feels when another enters his territory? Out of the corner of his eyes, he saw Ramona approaching. She came to a stop near him and listened.

"It would really mean a lot to me if you'd let me stay for a few days," Quinn said. "I promise I wouldn't be a bother."

Caitlin considered the man before her, thinking that it was too bad she was going to have to turn him down. He seemed charming, and his charm was inherent, not forced. She liked him for that. "Mr. O'Neill—"

His smile told her he knew what she was about to say. "You're going to break my heart if you say no."

She laughed ruefully. "You're not making this easy for me."

"Good. Then you'll let me stay?"

"Caitlin pretty much has her hands full," Nico said, speaking up for the first time. "A guest would be out of the question."

"He's right—" she began.

"What's one more person?" Ramona asked.

All three turned toward her in surprise.

Ramona shrugged, uncomfortable beneath the scrutiny. "Heaven knows we have plenty of space, and I always cook for twenty anyway. And you can charge him enough to cover the cost of those new draperies you're going to have to order."

"Ramona's obviously bored," Caitlin said to Nico, her tone wry. "Taking care of you and me has lost its challenge."

"I thought you were going to Boston," Nico said pointedly to Ramona.

"Plans can be changed," she said just as pointedly as she crossed the marble floor to them. "Besides, Mr. O'Neill said he only planned to stay for a few days, and Boston will still be there when I get ready to go. Mr. O'Neill, I'm Ramona Johnson."

Quinn stepped forward and took her hand. "It's a pleasure to meet you. And thank you."

"Nothing to thank me for. Caitlin's is the final decision."

"Are you sure about this, Ramona?" Caitlin asked, and at Ramona's nod, she spread her hands. "Well, if you won't mind the mess, Mr. O'Neill, and Ramona doesn't mind the extra work, I don't suppose there's any reason why you can't stay."

"Thank you, Caitlin," he said seriously. "I'll try not to do anything that would make you regret your decision."

Ramona spoke up. "We'll choose you a bedroom, Mr. O'Neill, and then you can help me prepare it. Caitlin, have you moved your things yet?"

"Not yet, but I will."

"Are you going to need any assistance?"

"I don't think so. Thank you anyway."

"I'll show you the way, Mr. O'Neill."

"Quinn, please."

Nico's gaze followed the two as they ascended the stairs, Quinn moving easily beside Ramona. He was in good condition, Nico reflected, his body lean and muscled. And the uneasy feeling persisted that there was more to Quinn O'Neill than what he'd told Caitlin.

Is he the man Rettig has sent after me, he wondered grimly.

Six

Gossamer curtains of mist drifted across the cliffs. The sounds of the ocean and the gulls were loud in the early-morning quiet.

Quinn watched Caitlin, as he had ever since he'd arrived two days ago, and thought again how lovely she was. Wearing a flowing white dress, she seemed as ethereal as the diaphanous white haze through which she walked.

"Good morning, Caitlin," he called when she drew close enough to hear him.

"Good morning. I didn't know anyone else was up yet."

"At six a.m., no matter where I am in the world, my eyes pop open. What's your excuse?"

She laughed. "I've always loved this time of day on the cliffs. Even when I was a little girl, I used to climb out of bed and come here. I considered this time and this place my very own piece of heaven before the day began. I never grew out of that feeling. And now with the work going on at the house, I steal this time before the workmen start arriving at eight."

Quinn's expression turned rueful. "And here I've intruded. I'm sorry."

"Oh no, don't be. Actually, I'm glad I ran into you. I didn't see you yesterday. I have a feeling you're taking pains to keep out of the way."

"You were kind enough to let me stay. The least I can do in return is try not to be a bother."

She studied him curiously. "Tell me, has being back at SwanSea lived up to your expectations, or are you disappointed?"

He smiled slowly. "My expectations have been more than fulfilled."

"I'm glad."

"How is your family these days? I've heard rumblings that your uncle Seldon, Senator Deverell, is contemplating a bid for the presidency."

She laughed. "That's right. If he decides to go for it, the experts say he'll win. And Uncle Jacob still holds the title of chairman of the board, but his son Conall pretty much runs Deverell's these days."

"And your mother?"

"She's fine. She's away at the moment."

After a moment, Quinn said, "I think your grandfather made a very wise decision to leave SwanSea to you, Caitlin."

Through the shifting veils of mist, she stared at the house. "Grandfather said that since I was the only Deverell ever to have been born here, I had an extraordinary bond to the house. SwanSea has always been special to the Deverells, but he felt that I was the only one of his four children and two grandchildren who could see what my great-grandfather Edward saw in it. Maybe it was because I spent so many years alone here with only my mother, Ramona, and the house for company. The house was almost like a playmate."

"And now you're taking steps to share it with others," Quinn said gently. "That is admirable."

She shrugged. "Not really. My decision involves many things."

"But I'm willing to bet that at the bottom of all those reasons is love of SwanSea."

She nodded and looked back at him. "Sometime I'd like you to tell me about the time you spent here. I enjoy hearing stories about how it used to be."

He turned slightly, so that his expression was partially obscured. "SwanSea's future will shine every bit as bright as its past, Caitlin. I'm confident. Look, there's a fishing boat. Makes a pretty picture, doesn't it, coming out of the mist like that."

She followed his gaze. "It's riding low in the water. I guess they've already gotten their catch. They must have been out for a few days."

From his bedroom window, Nico also stared at the fishing boat. He'd seen it before, and something about it bothered him, although he couldn't decide what. His gaze returned to Caitlin and the man she was talking to.

Quinn O'Neill disturbed him too. A lot. If he'd known when he'd felt Caitlin slip out of bed earlier that she would run into Quinn, he would have gone with her. He felt no sense of security that this was the start of Quinn's second full day here and so far he had made no overt moves. Quinn was watching him just as he was watching Quinn. Maybe he was exactly what he seemed, but Nico seriously doubted it. But whatever and whoever Quinn was, he could handle him.

Caitlin was another matter. Nico had no confidence that their situation would be as simple. She'd not only trusted him into her home; now she'd trusted him into her bed. There were times when he felt like the lowest of the low, a first-class bastard. But at night, when they made love, he forgot everything but her. And despite his guilty conscience, whether it was daylight or dark, he knew he'd do everything in his power, honest or dishonest, to keep her with him.

With fresh determination when Caitlin was busy, he had intensified his search of the attic, the most likely place where something from long ago would have been stored.

But he'd made a crucial decision. He could no longer go on without telling Caitlin. He didn't want to hurt her. And no matter her reaction, he didn't want to deceive her.

The mist was lifting; the sun was coming out. Quinn and Caitlin were walking toward the house. Nico's mouth curved with a tender smile as he looked down on Caitlin. No, he thought. He didn't want to hurt her. He wanted only to love her.

Clusters of glass grapes hung from the ceiling at different lengths in a fantasy grape arbor created by Louis Comfort Tiffany. Each cluster sheathed a light and cast a iridescent glow over Nico's bedroom that evening. Fresh from the shower, he lay across the end of the bed, his elbow propping up his head, a towel draped over his hips.

A few feet away, Caitlin swept a silver-backed brush through her hair. Her every movement caused light to flow through the folds of the pale gold silk nightgown.

"I can't believe that one hundred rolls of wallpaper

were delivered today and not one of them was the right pattern," she was saying.

"Why can't you believe it?" he asked absently, enthralled by her feminine rituals. Each pass of the brush through her hair brought more life and luster to the long strands.

She paused, giving his question thought. "I don't know. I suppose I expected that because it was SwanSea being renovated, everyone involved would give their all." Unexpectedly, the sound of her laughter erupted, spreading a warmth through the room and him. "I guess it was a pretty absurd assumption on my part, wasn't it?"

"I don't think you were that far off base. The men who you have working for you seem very conscientious."

"They are. But then, most of them have grown up around here, and they have relatives who've worked for the family. Some even have ancestors who helped build the house. But the supplies I'm dealing with long-distance have never seen SwanSea."

"It will all work out," he said softly.

"I know. And we do have the electricity back."

"I didn't mind using candles."

"I didn't either, now that you mention it." The smile she gave him spoke of a sexual familiarity, and it sent desire tingling through him. Any second now, his decision would become secondary to his desire, and he couldn't let that happen.

"There is something I have to tell you, Caitlin."

She tossed the brush onto a chair, pushed him back on the bed, and slid on top of him, arranging herself so that she lay full length over him. She dropped a kiss on his mouth, then crossing her arms on his chest, she propped her chin on her arms. "You're frowning. Why?"

"Because of what I have to tell you." He smiled with regret. "And Caitlin, I can only think of one thing when you're on top of me."

"What's so bad about that?" she asked and pressed a kiss on his chin.

"Not a damn thing. But . . ." He shifted out from under her, took a pair of shorts from the wardrobe, and slipped them on.

She sat up and eyed him worriedly. "Whatever this is, it must be bad if you have to get dressed."

His lips twisted. "I'm getting dressed because with the two of us wearing little or nothing, I can't forget, even for a few minutes, how very much I want you."

She sighed. "Okay, Nico, what is it?"

He braced his hands on his hips, searching his mind for some way to make the next few minutes easier for both of them. But there was no way. "Caitlin, I want you to know that I've systematically searched quite a bit of your house. In fact, I chose SwanSea as a place to recuperate because of my search."

The color in her face slowly drained away. *"What?"*

"It's true," he said grimly. "In fact, you caught me in the act one day as I was looking through the desk in the study. Remember?"

"Yes, but you said you were writing a letter to your great-grandmother and you needed a pen."

"A story I had prepared, just in case someone walked in and found me."

She couldn't begin to guess what he was leading up to, but she knew if it were bad, she was vulnerable. Her love for him had left her wide open. But this couldn't be as bad as it sounded, she thought, refusing to jump to any conclusions. "I don't understand what it is you're trying to tell me."

"Just wait. I'm afraid your confusion is going to

get worse. I'd do anything to spare us this, but from this moment on, I'm resolved there will be no more secrets between us."

"You're scaring me, Nico."

He knelt in front of the bed and took her hand. "Don't be afraid. What I'm about to tell you, Caitlin, holds importance only for people long dead and one very sick old woman. Try to remember that."

"All right."

"This concerns your great-grandfather Edward and his firstborn son and legitimate heir, John—my great-grandfather."

"Your *what?*" Shock made her whisper.

His lips briefly compressed. "I understand how hard this must be for you, but hear me out. I told you that Elena is ill and that lately she'd been speaking to me of a time long ago when she was a young woman in Italy. One night, right before I was shot, I made one of my regular visits to her, and she told me something I'd never heard before. In fact, none of the family had ever heard this story. It was so fantastic, we weren't even sure it was true. We're still not."

"What did she tell you?"

"The young man she met and married in 1916, when she was seventeen years old, was John Deverell."

She looked at him oddly. "John died in the war. That's why Edward sought out grandfather." She thought for a minute. "You think John and Elena married?"

"I'm only telling you what Elena told me. Do you know any details about John?"

"No, not really. I'm not sure anyone in the family does."

"Well, the DiFrenzas have never known anything except that Elena's husband was named John. She told me the rest of the story that night. In 1913, when John was eighteen, he left America to go on a grand tour. I gather there were some problems with his father, but she wasn't specific. The war began to break out in Europe, country by country, but John didn't want to return home. He liked being independent. Eventually, he must have been caught up in the fervor of the war because he enlisted in the Italian underground where he was really out of his father's reach. He and Elena met and married, and not too much longer after that, in 1917, he was killed. According to Elena, Edward knew nothing about her or her marriage to John, or that before his death, they had conceived a child. When the child was born, Elena named him Giovanni—John. My grandfather."

Caitlin could only stare at him, staggered by what she was hearing.

"Europe had been ravaged by the war," he said, "and Elena, all alone with her infant son, wrote to Edward of her marriage to John and of the child. She entered her son's name in her family Bible beneath his father's signature, inserted her letter of explanation between its pages along with her marriage certificate, wrapped up the Bible and mailed it off to America. John had told her his father was a hard man, but Elena was confident that with the documentation she was sending him, he wouldn't ignore the fact that he had a grandson, that he would send for them as soon as he received the package. Days turned into months and months into years, and Elena never heard from Edward."

"Why?" Caitlin asked. "Assuming all of this was true, of course."

"I have no idea. Neither does she. But she told me she was so angry and hurt that she took back her maiden name. And after several years, she was able to save money for passage to America. The rest of the story my family knew. She started out sewing in one of those sweatshops, making clothes for a local manufacturer. But she was smart, and through hard work and luck, she was able to open a little shop of her own. That shop's success eventually led to what is known today as DiFrenza's."

"But if she was so angry, why did she move to the same city Edward lived in?"

He grinned. "If you knew Elena, you'd know that's something she'd do. She's a tiny thing, but she's got enough stubbornness and pride for a dozen big men. She told me she'd never attempted to contact any Deverell, though there must have been times when she could have used an influential and powerful ally. In fact, she told me that all these years, she's viewed the Deverell name with great disdain. She said if they didn't want her in their family, she certainly didn't want them in hers." His grin faded. "But she does want back the Bible that lists the birth of her son along with the signature of her husband."

She gazed at him, her mind whirling.

"After I was shot, I decided to use my convalescent period to ease her mind, come up here, and poke around a bit. Besides that, my captain was urging me to get out of town." Watching her, Nico saw an array of emotions reflected on her face. He'd confessed the most important part of his subterfuge, and he hoped she still trusted him. Unfortunately he didn't have a clue as to what she was feeling.

"Nico, why didn't you tell me all of this when you first came here, instead of the lies and the searching behind my back?"

He'd been waiting for the question, and he had no thought of trying to duck it. "Caitlin, what would you have done if I'd shown up on your doorstep and announced that I had a contract on my head, needed a place to recuperate from bullet wounds given to me by a drug lord, and oh, by the way, it was possible that I was related to your family, but I needed to search the house to find the proof."

"I would have slammed the door in your face."

"Right."

"But after we got to know one another—"

"Remember, I wasn't sure if the story was true. I didn't want you to think that I had been using you or that I was trying to take something away from you."

"You did use me," she pointed out with unerring reason.

He was a brave man; courage came easily to him. But telling her the truth about what he'd done had proved to be one of the hardest things he'd ever had to do. The thought that he might lose her made his nerves unsteady. "You have to understand that I deal with life-and-death situations on a daily basis, and this seemed harmless in comparison. Initially I was using you, but I knew my intentions were only to put Elena's mind to rest, not to harm you in any way. And if it makes you feel any better, I started feeling guilty as hell almost immediately."

"But not enough to tell me?"

She wasn't going to be able to understand, he thought, then quickly shook his despair away. No. She *had* to understand, and she *had* to forgive him. He wouldn't let her out of this room until she did.

He rose from his knees and sat beside her on the bed, turning to face her. "By then, I had too much to lose if you didn't believe me. So I put off telling you. And put it off. And put it off. I haven't handled any of this worth a damn, Caitlin. I admit it. I'm a bastard. But I'm a bastard who loves you. No matter what, always remember that."

She felt the breath leave her body. "You love me?"

"More than my own life."

She could hardly believe her ears. "You love me? Why haven't you told me?"

All the love and tenderness he felt for her showed in his smile. "I fought like hell not to love you, but I think I was lost the first minute I laid eyes on you." He paused. "Caitlin, what do you think about what I've just told you about Elena and John?"

"I don't know what to think," she said truthfully. "As a matter of fact, I'm finding it very hard to think at all at the moment." Suddenly she laughed and threw her arms around his neck. "You love me," she said, her voice filled with amazement.

He groaned. "Caitlin, we need to talk more about the Bible and letter I've been searching for."

She put a hand to his face. "Nico, it's natural for me to be astonished by this news. Anyone would feel the same if they had just been told there might be a whole new line to their family tree. But why should we waste any more time talking about something that might not even be true? Especially since I have something very important to tell you."

"Caitlin—"

"I love you, Nico."

He stared at her, stunned. "Do you mean that, or are you just saying it?"

She laughed joyously. "Why would I say something like that if I didn't mean it?"

Bewildered, he raked his hands through his hair. "I don't know."

"Don't you want me to love you?"

"*Want* you to love me? Caitlin—"

The look of utter wonderment on his face made her act. She stood and gracefully shimmied out of the pale gold silk gown until she stood naked before him. "Make love to me, Nico."

With a low, rough sound of surrender, he reached for her and pulled her down beside him. The lights above them filtered through the colored translucent glass, casting the shapes and deep rose-and-purple colors of grapes over her skin. His mouth began to water as his body hardened.

He bent to taste the wine of the grapes.

Seven

His room had been searched. Nico knew it as soon as he entered his room the next afternoon after a jog. Nothing was out of place; nothing seemed disturbed. But his sixth sense was telling him that his room had been gone through in an extremely professional manner.

Quinn O'Neill. It couldn't be anyone else.

Ever since he'd been here, the work crew has been in and out of the house, and nothing unusual had happened. Besides, Caitlin knew them all. Quinn was the stranger at SwanSea.

He'd already considered the idea that Quinn could be after him. What he hadn't considered was that Quinn could be after Caitlin. It was time to act.

He made a quick trip outside, but Quinn's car was gone. Back upstairs, he called Amarillo.

"I need you to do something for me," he said as soon as he heard his friend on the line.

"Does it involve killing someone?" Amarillo asked with mild interest.

Nico's lips quirked. This was just one of the many

times Nico had been thankful that Amarillo was on his side. "I'm not sure yet. Depends on what you find. A man by the name of Quinn O'Neill has shown up here. Use every contact you have, call in favors, beg if you have to, but find out who he is."

"What's he done?"

"My room's been searched. I'm sure he found my badge and gun."

Amarillo's laconic tone disappeared. "Get out of there now, Nico. Your position's been compromised. I told you two days ago that I have a safe place up the coast all ready for you."

"I can't leave him here with Caitlin until I know who he is. Besides, I don't think he's after me. If he was, he would have been supplied with positive identification, photos, the works. But if he's after Caitlin, he might have searched my room to find out who I was and what sort of threat I might be to his plans."

"You mean because he's seen the two of you together?"

"Right."

"I don't like this one bit, Nico."

"Believe me, I'm not jumping for joy myself, but I'll argue with you later. For now, do as I ask. He's driven off somewhere, so I don't have his license number, but here's his description."

Caitlin's face lit up when she saw Nico walk into her study. "I've been wondering where you were and what you were doing."

He leaned across the desk and gave her a kiss. "And I've been wondering how you and I can pull an escape."

"An escape?"

"How would you like to get away from the house

for a while? Take a drive. See a movie. Eat lunch somewhere. *Anything.* I'm open to suggestion as long as it's away from here."

She grinned. "Feeling cooped up?"

He straightened. "I'm not sure 'cooped up' is the right phrase. After all, SwanSea is bigger than some countries."

"Not quite," she said with a laugh.

"Well, almost. But I'm definitely restless and in the mood to see something different."

She glanced at the mound of paperwork on her desk and grimaced.

"There's nothing there that can't wait, Caitlin."

Making an instant decision, she pushed away from the desk and stood up. "You're absolutely right. How about going into town? I'd love to show it to you, and I know a great place for lunch."

"Sounds good."

She clapped her hands together, excited. "Okay, now all we have to do is get out of here without anyone stopping me to ask a question."

"Walk fast, don't meet anyone's eyes, and keep a straight face. With any luck, we'll be out of here before anyone notices you're gone."

"Good plan. I approve."

Two people called out to her and they received more than a few strange looks, but no one tried to stop them. And by the time they reached the front veranda, their obvious furtiveness had reduced them to giggles.

"We made it," she said joyfully.

Nico's laughter faded as he saw Quinn coming up the steps toward them. "Not quite."

Quinn nodded coolly to Nico, but gave Caitlin a smile. "Hello. What are you two up to?"

"We're running away for the afternoon," Caitlin

said in a conspiratorial tone. "But you've got to promise not to tell anyone."

He crossed his heart solemnly. "I promise. Are you running away to any place in particular or just running?"

"Just running," Nico said, not wanting to reveal to Quinn where they'd be.

"We're going into town," Caitlin said.

Quinn shot Nico a look that set off alarm bells in his head. One thing was for sure. Quinn didn't trust Nico any more than Nico trusted him. The search of his room proved that if nothing else. But why?

"I've just returned from there," Quinn said, speaking to Caitlin. "It's a charming place, and I have to say it hasn't changed all that much since the last time I was here."

"When exactly *was* that?" Nico asked. "I don't believe you ever said."

Quinn gave a self deprecating laugh. "That's because I can't remember. Over the years, my sense of time has become warped."

"What did you do in town?" Caitlin asked.

"Nothing much. Just wandered around. Revisited some of the places I had seen so long ago."

"And it really hasn't changed?" she asked.

"Not in any significant way. Oh, I think there've been one or two coats of paint added, and of course the church is finished now. But it looked to me as if the same families were running the same shops. The fudge even tasted the same. Sinful."

Caitlin laughed. "Ah, you visited the candy store. We'll have to do that too," she told Nico. "The fudge they make there is to die for."

The phrase sent a chill up his spine. "We'd better get going," Nico said quietly.

• • •

"You've been awfully quiet," Caitlin said, studying Nico. "Are you upset about something?"

Silently, wearily, he cursed himself. He had forgotten how perceptive she could be. He'd been thinking about Quinn and wondering why he had searched his room. "No, I'm not upset, but I am sorry. I guess I haven't been very good company."

They'd chosen to eat in a converted boathouse at the end of a long pier. Inside the rustic restaurant, old copper gleamed, and lobster traps adorned the walls. Their table was covered by plastic-coated oil-cloth and was set by a big picture window. The ocean surrounded them and rolled beneath them.

"You don't have to be good company, Nico," Caitlin said. "Just being with you is enough to make me happy."

His dark eyes narrowed on her. "Has anyone ever told you that you're wonderful?"

She tried unsuccessfully to swallow a sudden lump. "Right at this moment, I can't remember a time."

"Then let me tell you. You're wonderful."

"You're going to make me blush."

He propped his arms on the table and took her hand. "I like it when you blush all over."

"I *don't* blush all over. Maybe a little bit on the cheekbones, but definitely not all over."

"You do, and I'll prove it to you tonight. All I have to do is start kissing you on your—"

"Do you have everything you need?"

They both started and broke away. A small tow-headed boy about five years old was standing by their table.

"My mom sent me over to ask you. She said to say it just like how I said it."

Caitlin smiled. "Hi, Tommy. You know I almost didn't recognize you, you're getting to be so big."

He nodded solemnly. "I know." He stuck his hands deep into the pockets of his overalls and looked at Nico. "Do you want some of my grandma's blueberry cobbler? It's real good. She baked two panfuls this morning."

"Really? And you recommend this cobbler, do you?"

The boy nodded. "I've already had a bowl. I wanted another, but my mom said no."

Nico grinned. "I guess that's a pretty good recommendation. I'll take a bowl. How about you, Caitlin?"

"Sure, why not? What's an extra five pounds or so?"

"You have to have it with ice cream," Tommy said, " 'cause it's better that way."

"We'll trust your judgment," Nico said.

Caitlin groaned. "Make that ten pounds."

Tommy smiled from ear to ear. "I'll go tell my mom."

"Cute kid," Nico said.

"Precious," she said. "As you may have gathered, this is a family business. Tommy's brothers caught the lobster that went into our stew, and his father cooked it."

"It was delicious."

Caitlin took a spoon and crushed a silver-dollar-size mint leaf against the side of her tea glass. "You were good with him. Did you ever think you'd like to have children?"

He arched an eyebrow in surprise. "No, not really. Police work is hard on family life."

"But it doesn't make it impossible. And I gather your family is very important to you."

"Very," he said with a smile. "In fact, that's something you and I have in common."

"It's true. Although physically my family is pretty far-flung most of the time, we are very close."

He hesitated, then proceeded carefully. "Except, apparently, for one member."

She looked puzzled. "Who?"

"Your father. I've been wondering about him."

She shrugged. "I've never had one, except biologically of course."

"What happened? Did he leave you and your mother when you were a baby?"

"Try before I was born. It was a hit-and-run sort of affair."

He reached over and clasped her hand in his. "That sounds very bitter. Was it hard on you growing up without a father?"

"No, of course not. I couldn't miss something I never had."

"I'm not sure I believe that."

She grimaced. "Well, to tell you the truth, I'm not sure I do either. But my mother suffered more than I did, though she never said anything."

"Do you mind talking about this?"

"Not with you. I've never felt the stigma of being illegitimate. It wasn't the badge of dishonor it was in grandfather's day."

"Then why did you and your mother live in such seclusion and isolation at SwanSea for the first six years of your life?"

"I think she needed those years to come to terms with what had happened. And we weren't always alone. The family visited often."

"And you loved having SwanSea all to yourself."

She flashed him a grin. "I did, but looking back on it, I can see that Mother was in pain. I guess that's what I resent my unknown father for most— what he did to my mother. *Anyway*," she said brightly, "that's all in the past, and there's something I've been wondering about that very much concerns the present."

"What's that?"

"Well, it's obvious that you're almost fully recovered now."

"I *am* recovered," he said firmly.

She nodded. "Well, I've been thinking about your work and wondering how much longer you can stay."

"Anxious to get rid of me?" he asked, mentally running through his situation. There was still the matter of Nathan Rettig. He was out there somewhere, searching for him. And then there was Quinn. He wasn't about to leave Caitlin alone until he had figured out who Quinn was and what he wanted.

The wry face she made was an attempt to cover her self-consciousness. He'd told her he loved her, but he'd offered no commitment. "You know better than that."

He stood, leaned across the table, and kissed her in full view of the other patrons. Then he sat back down and took her hand again. "I know your work is here and mine is in Boston. I'm not sure how, Caitlin, but we'll work it out. There's no way I'm letting you get away from me. No way."

Until the real thing came along, she thought, she'd take that as a commitment. Reassured, Caitlin smiled, and when Tommy's mother set their ice-cream-ladened cobblers in front of them, she gave a carefree laugh. "This blows my plans to have fudge for dessert."

A half hour later, the warm afternoon breeze rippled the surface of the small deep-water harbor, making the masted sailboats bob and the water glisten like a black-green jewel. Robin's-egg blue, sunshine-yellow, forest-green, and deep-red colors adorned the clapboard buildings with their steeply pitched roofs and their geranium-filled window boxes.

"The candy shop is just up ahead," Caitlin said, her arm in Nico's.

"How can you be interested in fudge after that lunch we just had?" He reached down and patted her flat stomach. "Where do you put it all?"

She laughed. "I'm not saying I want to eat the fudge now. But they sell fudge *to go.*" She lifted her eyebrows in what was meant to be a significant manner.

He smiled indulgently. Caitlin in a playful mood had a way of melting away his problems. "Ah, I see. *To go.*"

"Right. We can get a bag and take it back with us. For *tonight.*"

"You and fudge," he murmured. "I can hardly wait."

In a show of mock dismay, she hit her forehead with the heel of her hand. "Oh, no! What am I going to do if you find out that you like the fudge better than you like me?"

The look he gave her was potent with love and wanting. "Not a chance."

"You haven't tasted this fudge yet," she said softly.

"No, but I've tasted you."

"Taste me again," she whispered, leaning against him.

He groaned and bent his head to brush her lips, then dip his tongue into her mouth.

"Let's go home," he murmured.

She felt a small thrill at the fact that he'd unconsciously referred to SwanSea as home. "We will as soon as we get our fudge. Besides, we're here."

"Here?"

"Here," she said, motioning toward a large plate-glass window. "Look, he's about to make a new batch."

On the other side of the window, a pleasant-faced rotund man poured hot fudge onto a cool marble slab.

"That's Paul McGruder," she said, waving to the man. "He owns the shop."

She leaned back against Nico, and he circled his arms around her waist. While they watched, Paul took up a scraper and began lifting the rich dark chocolate and folding it back on itself. He repeated the process again and again.

"Why do I think you've spent a lot of time in front of this window?" Nico asked, his mouth to her ear.

"I have no idea why you would think that." Her tone was innocent, but her expression was rapt.

As the fudge began to thicken, Paul reached for a handful of walnuts and sprinkled them over the glistening surface of the candy. Knowing that he had an audience, he performed his tasks with flourish, slicing through the nuts with the scraper to mix them into the fudge.

Images flowed across the plate-glass window— people strolling behind them along the harbor's edge, the boats, a dog chasing a low-flying bird.

But it was Caitlin's reflection that Nico studied in the glass, enjoying her delight in the candy making. Over the past days, he'd learned that there were many sides to her: the woman who was wild and passionate in his bed, the dreamer and the businesswoman who was bringing SwanSea back to life, the playful flirt, and now the little girl who loved to watch fudge being made. *He loved all the Caitlins.*

"If we don't go home immediately," he whispered in her ear, "I'm going to make love to you right here."

The next afternoon, Nico surveyed the attic room he had been methodically searching for the last two hours. Caitlin now knew what he was doing and why, but he wasn't at all happy about his activities, and he'd made a vow to himself. There were more attic rooms, but this was the last he planned to go through.

He believed the rambling story Elena had told him; he'd made her a promise, and he'd tried to fulfill that promise to the best of his ability. But he owed Caitlin his loyalty. And this would be the last time he would dig through her family's possessions. His investigation ended here.

Without enthusiasm, he knelt before yet another dusty trunk and inserted a pick into the old lock, gently manipulating the rusty mechanism until it sprang open. Lifting the lid, he delved into the contents.

Quilts, old letters, shoes, lace, odds and ends. He had pulled half the contents onto the floor when he saw the package. Wrapped in plain brown paper and tied with string, the package bore a postmark more than seventy years old.

"Oh, hell," he murmured.

With the minimum of tearing and ripping, he slipped off the string and the paper, then let out a long shaky breath as he stared at the contents of the package. "Oh, *hell*," he said again, this time with force and meaning.

Reluctantly, he checked the entry in the Bible and scanned the marriage license. He'd found the proof Elena wanted.

For one wild moment, he was tempted to destroy it, he was so concerned about how Caitlin would take the news. They'd both become distracted last night, and he hadn't had a chance to say everything he had planned to say.

Reason, plus loyalty and love for Elena, quickly reasserted themselves. The news would make Elena happy. Whatever other waves the news created, he vowed, he was going to move heaven and earth to make sure that nothing changed between him and Caitlin

Slowly, he replaced the contents of the trunk along with the package, shut the lid, and went to find her.

"Hi," Caitlin said, meeting Nico just outside her study. "I was coming to find you."

"Through with your work?"

She nodded.

"Good, because—"

"Nico?" Ramona called, coming down the hall "There's a phone call for you."

"You can take it in my study," Caitlin said. "I'l wait for you in the drawing room."

"No." He took her hand. "I don't mind you being there."

In the study, he picked up the phone. "Rill?"

"Yeah. I'm afraid I've got some bad news. I've just been notified that two of Rettig's men were spotted in your area."

"*Damn.*"

"Now listen. The local police may be first rate for all I know, and we'll fill them in out of courtesy, but I want our people to handle this."

"I agree."

"Good. Stay put. I'll be there in—"

"Hold it. Let's think this through before we jump the gun. If they've found me, why haven't they acted?"

"I don't know," Amarillo said tightly, "but if it will make you feel any better, I'll ask them right after I cuff them."

Nico glanced at Caitlin and saw her gazing at him anxiously. He pulled her against him. "Give me to-night, Rill, and I'll call you tomorrow." A long stretch of silence followed. "I mean it, Rill."

"You're taking a big chance, Nico."

"I know, but I'm not the only one involved."

"You mean Caitlin? We can protect her too."

"We may have to, but I want more information before I make a decision. Something's not right. Have you gotten that other information I wanted?"

"Give me a call back in an hour. I should have it by then."

"Good, because I'll be basing my decision on it."

Nico hung up the phone and looked at her.

"What is it?"

He leaned back on the desk, pulled her between his outstretched legs, and began the story. "The name of the man I was investigating before he shot me is Nathan Rettig. I've just been told that two of his men have been spotted in the area. I have to assume they've tracked me here."

"Nico, no—"

"Don't worry. They're obviously waiting for something. Perhaps Rettig himself. I'm something he wouldn't want to leave to his minions. I've been able to heavily curtail his operation, although I haven't been able to get anything to stick. I'm like a thorn in his side, and he wants me bad."

"Maybe their being in the village is a coincidence," she said, clutching at straws.

"There are no coincidences where Rettig and his men are concerned. If it's not me that's brought them to the village, it's something to do with drug trafficking. Hell, for all I know, it could be both me and the drugs. But whatever the reason, I've got to find out."

"Leave it alone, Nico. Let someone else go after him this time."

He felt an incredible sadness as he met her troubled gaze. He knew he couldn't do as she asked, and he didn't even want to.

She read his thoughts and wrapped her arms around herself to still the shudder she could feel spreading in her. Nico in danger hadn't been a reality to her before now.

His hand strayed to the side of her head and brushed a silky wave. "I'm so sorry, honey."

"For what?" she asked, startled.

"For bringing danger into your safe world. I never meant to, you've got to believe me."

"I do."

"But you're scared."

"Yes," she said in a small voice.

"It's nothing to be ashamed of. When you've lived all your life in safety, it's hard to cope with danger, except in the abstract. Try not to worry. I'm going to do everything in my power to make sure the danger doesn't touch you."

"And what are you going to do to protect yourself?"

He smiled. "The same. Everything in my power. I don't have a death wish, Caitlin. Especially now that I've found you."

She felt her eyes fill with tears and blinked them away. "So what are your plans?"

"I should get out of here, but there's someone here at SwanSea I don't trust, and I'm too concerned about you to leave just yet."

"Me?"

"Caitlin, it's Quinn O'Neill."

"Quinn?" she asked, surprised.

"He disturbs me. He seems to watch you all the time. But there are other things. For a retired man on vacation, he takes great care to blend into the woodwork. He watches, but he doesn't want anyone watching him."

"Maybe that's just his personality."

"I don't think so. But in any case, I thought you

should know. I'm having Rill, the man who just called, check him out right now. I'm only sorry I didn't do it the first day Quinn came here."

"Why didn't you if you were suspicious?"

"Because I was all tangled up with you," he said huskily, "and I couldn't be sure why my instincts were telling me to be on guard. I could have been just jealous of the man."

"Oh, Nico."

He put his arm around her, pressed his mouth to the top of her head, and breathed in the special scent that was Caitlin.

"Nico, I just thought of something!" She pulled away and looked up at him, her eyes wide with alarm. "When we met Quinn on the front veranda yesterday afternoon, he said the village hadn't changed much except for a few coats of paint and the fact that the church was finished."

"Go on."

"Mr. Haines mentioned the other day that they built the church twenty-five or twenty-six years ago. That means that Quinn must have been here during that time."

Nico nodded. "Sounds like it."

"But don't you see? He said he was here visiting Grandfather. Grandfather didn't live here during that time. He and Arabella were in Europe. The house was closed up."

"Are you sure?"

"Absolutely. Quinn lied to me."

Nico's mouth tightened. "Let's go for a walk. By the time we get back, Rill should have that information."

The sun was setting behind the great house, the color of the ocean darkening, but the scene was lost on the two men who stood on the bluff talking intently.

"So now you know," Quinn said, carefully watching Nico's face for reaction. "I thought I could come here, stay awhile, then leave without anyone being the wiser."

"That sounds familiar," Nico said. It was no wonder something in him had recognized that Quinn should be handled with care. The two of them were much alike.

Quinn slipped his hands into his trouser pockets and rocked back on his heels. "You have my life in your hands . . . so to speak. What are you going to do?"

"My main concern is that Caitlin not be hurt. If you leave now, she won't be."

"And if I do leave, I have your word that you'll keep silent?" Quinn asked without expression.

"You have my word."

"I wasn't ready to leave yet, but—"

"This afternoon would be a good time, but I'll accept in the morning."

Quinn studied Nico's hard face. He'd had many opportunities to observe him since he'd come to SwanSea, and he'd concluded that Nico was not a man he'd want to cross. But Nico was also a man he could admire without any reservations. A wry grin creased his face. "Your partner must have dug real deep to find me."

"There's nothing and no one Amarillo can't find if he sets his mind to it."

"Well, I'm going to have to make a few calls to see that it doesn't happen again."

"That might be a good idea."

Quinn nodded, knowing there was nothing left to say. He turned slightly, preparing to leave, when his attention was caught. "That's odd," he said.

"What?" Nico jerked his head around to the ocean and followed Quinn's gaze. "You mean that fishing boat?"

"Yes. It's riding low in the water, which should indicate they have their catch for the day. But there's no seagulls around the boat. Fish always draw seagulls."

"That *is* odd," Nico said thoughtfully.

When Caitlin had first rounded the corner of the house and seen Nico and Quinn out on the cliff, she'd had a sudden whimsical thought that she was viewing a scene out of an old western. The two men were standing as if they were facing off, their postures radiating tension. She'd wondered if her intrusion would defuse the situation or make it worse. In the end, she'd decided to let the two men play it out themselves, and as she watched, she saw the tension gradually fade away.

As he walked back to the house, Quinn saw Caitlin, hesitated, then continued toward her. "Caitlin, I'm glad to see you. I was on my way to find you."

"Oh?"

His composure faltered only slightly in the face of her obvious coolness. "I wanted to personally thank you for allowing me to stay at SwanSea. I plan to thank Ramona too, of course."

She glanced over his shoulder to the cliff and Nico, then looked back at him. "Then you're leaving?"

"Yes, I'm afraid I have to. I'll pack tonight and start out in the morning, but I probably won't see you again before I go."

She didn't know whether Nico was still suspicious of Quinn, but his leaving was probably best. Still, she was curious. "Do you plan to continue your vacation somewhere else?"

"I think I've had enough vacation for a while. I

need to get on with my retirement plans—decide what I'm going to do with the rest of my life."

She brushed a strand of hair from her eyes. "You know, you really don't look old enough to retire."

Without waiting for her to offer her hand, he reached out and took it. "Thank you. That's a very nice compliment, but I'm ready to retire, believe me. And I just want to say that it was a pleasure meeting you. You're a lovely young woman. Good-bye, Caitlin."

"Good-bye." She stared after him, wondering why she felt disturbed about his leaving. She felt the warmth of Nico's body behind her and turned to look up at him. "Quinn says he's going in the morning. Did he tell you?"

"Yes."

"Well? Tell me what happened. What did you find out about him?"

"I was wrong. He's not a problem or a threat to us."

Her gaze strayed in the direction Quinn had gone. Something about him troubled her, but she didn't know what. "Are you sure?"

"Yes, I'm sure."

"But what about the timing of his other stay here?"

"He said himself he couldn't remember exactly. He must have been mistaken about the church."

"I suppose that's possible. That was a long time ago, and he's apparently traveled much of the world. He's bound to have seen a lot of churches."

He made an abrupt gesture with his hand. "Well, at any rate, I'm not worried about Quinn anymore, but I am still worried about Rettig. I need to leave, Caitlin."

"Oh, no." She reached out for him. Her hand found the solid strength of his chest. "Please don't go."

He covered her hand with his. "I have to, Caitlin.

If Rettig knows where I am, my leaving will draw him away from here and you. If he doesn't know, it will eliminate the possibility that he'll find out."

He was a man accustomed to action and danger, she thought, but she wasn't. She loved him, and the thought that someone wanted to hurt him was unbearable. "I'm afraid for you."

He smiled with understanding. She'd never be afraid for herself. "I'll be safer away from here, Caitlin. If I stayed, my main concern would be you."

"Instead of watching out for yourself."

He nodded. He knew from the resignation in her voice that he'd given her the one argument she wouldn't try to take apart.

Her shoulders slumped. "Then I guess I'll have to let you go, won't I?"

He drew her to him until he could feel her soft curves against him. "We're going to be all right, Caitlin. I promise you. We're going to be all right."

The wind took his words, mixed them with the sound of the sea, and carried them up to the cloud that drifted across the sun and shadowed SwanSea.

Eight

Caitlin held a match to the wick of the last tall cream-colored candle. When the flame burned steadily, she turned.

Nico lay waiting for her on the bed. The pale white-gold light flowed over the muscular angles and planes of his masculine nudity, giving his skin the texture of velvet and muting the two red scars on his left side.

"Don't come back to me with any more scars," she whispered.

"I won't." He studied the way the candlelight behind her shone through the gold of her long silk gown, outlining her shape, making her appear at once dreamlike and incredibly desirable. "You're beautiful."

"I'm serious, Nico."

"Does that mean you wouldn't want me to come back to you if I happened to take another bullet?"

"I couldn't bear it."

"What?"

"If you didn't come back to me." Her strained voice betrayed the fragile state of her nerves.

In one fluid motion, he rose from the bed and went to her, framing her face between his hands. "I'll come back, Caitlin. There aren't enough bullets in the world to stop me."

"Promise me."

"I promise."

He drew her to the bed and down to the satin coverlet until they lay side by side.

"Do you believe me?" he asked, smoothing her hair away from her face.

"Yes."

"From this moment on, the things I tell you will always be the truth. I will never intentionally hurt you. I will never lie to you."

She reached out and touched his face, then let her fingers slowly drift down the hard length of his arm to entwine with his. "I'm going to miss you so much."

"We won't be apart long—that's another promise. I have the feeling that this case is close to being solved. I feel it." He lifted their joined hands to his mouth, kissed the back of her fingertips, then laid her hand between them so that he could push the gold-silk strap from her shoulder. The gown loosened from her breast, and he brushed his fingers across the tops of the high flesh. "So soft," he murmured.

Heat trembled through her. "I didn't think it was possible to want someone the way I want you."

His eyes glittered with a dark fire, and he bent his head to suck a silk-covered nipple to life. His loins ached for her, as did his heart. But now was for finding new ways to make love to her, for driving himself inside her until he couldn't think, couldn't hear, couldn't see—then beginning again. Now was the time for making love to her until she asked him to stop. She'd never done that, he prayed she never would.

He pulled and tugged at the nipple with a gentle, persistent ferocity until she writhed against him, mindlessly, helplessly.

There was a thundering in her brain, a fire low in her belly. She reached between them to grasp him and heard him draw in a ragged breath. With a delicate pressure, she stroked his length. His hands clenched the sheets, but he said nothing. She continued experimenting, learning the pressure that would make him groan aloud, the caressing touch that would make him roll his head from side to side against the pillow.

It was a time of heated enchantment for her. But soon his body drew taut, and she heard thickly spoken words rumble up from his chest. "You'd better stop."

"I don't want to stop. I like the feel of you." The pad of her finger found a particularly interesting spot and lingered.

"Ah . . ." His body jerked. "Lord, Caitlin!" He took her wrist, stilling the excruciating and wondrous motion of her hand. "I can make you stop," he said raggedly.

"By holding my wrist?"

"No."

She felt him slip his hands beneath her gown and touch her in a knowing, caressing way that soon had her moving against him once again, this time more urgently. He'd turned the tables on her.

"You're amazing," she said, gasping. "Magical. You make me burn . . . want . . . instantly, with just a touch."

"That's good." He slid his finger over her moist soft flesh—rubbing, pressing.

"Yes." Her heart was pumping so hard she was barely able to breathe. "That's good . . . very good . . . and it's bad."

"Bad?" He kissed her neck, then closed his teeth around her earlobe and nibbled. "Surely not."

His breath was hot on her skin, fueling the flames rising within her. "Yes. Bad because you make me hurt so much for you. I get to the point where I'll do anything to have you inside me."

With fraying control, he glided his fingers into her.

She closed her eyes, savoring the sensation of hundreds of pleasures that throbbed, tingled, and pulsed.

"Are you at that point yet?" he asked, his mouth against her ear.

"Yes," she whispered in an agony of desire. "Oh, Nico, yes!"

"And what will you do?"

Her green-gold eyes were alight with an inner fever as she opened them and looked up at him. "Whatever you want."

A hard shudder ripped through him. "You don't have to do a thing. I'll take care of everything."

Holding her tightly, he rolled onto his back and lifted her over him. His strong arms supported her weight as she positioned herself and then slowly, softly slid down over him meausre by measure until they were completely joined. A hoarse sound of satisfaction wrenched from his chest.

Above him, Caitlin shifted, maneuvering him deeper inside her. Already she could feel herself beginning to pulse toward the brink of release, and she began to move. But his hands flexed tightly on her buttocks, forcing her to a slower rhythm, guiding her to rock against him, to make circling movements with her hips.

She tilted her head back and moaned, feeling as though the pleasure might split her apart. Both straps had dropped off her shoulder, and the top of her gold-silk gown had slipped down to the very edge of her nipples, barely covering the tips of the tight rosepeaks.

Looking up at her, Nico's breath caught at the incredibly erotic picture she made. Gold silk, ivory skin, cinnamon hair—surrounded by white-gold light. The sight almost pushed him over the edge, but with superhuman strength and resolve, he pulled back.

She could feel the moment for which she yearned approaching. She leaned down to him so that her hands were braced on either side of him. Her nipples broke free of the gown and pressed into the thick black hair of his chest. Her hair fell like an exotic concealing veil around them. "You feel like hard, hot satin inside me," she whispered.

Her words set him on fire, and the start of the tiny inner convulsions of the muscles surrounding him stole away his sanity. He pushed high into her and surrendered himself to the night, the candlelight, and her.

The mist began to lift from the sea at dawn. Nico observed the scene from the balcony of his bedroom. In a little while he would wake Caitlin and say good-bye. For now, though, he was content to watch the day appear little by little.

He didn't want to leave.

It was a given that he didn't want to say good-bye to Caitlin; every minute he spent away from her would be painful.

What surprised him was the realization that he was going to hate to leave SwanSea. He'd come to know all its odd little quirks, all its nooks and crannies, all the personalities the house could convey. He'd grown accustomed to this view—the rolling green lawn, the cliffs, the sea, the island, the boats . . . Hell. He was being ridiculous. How could you miss a house?

He'd feel better about leaving if he knew exactly what was going on with Rettig. If Rettig knew he was here at SwanSea, why hadn't he tried something? And if Rettig didn't know, then what the hell were his men doing in the area?

Nico frowned. Through the thinning mist he could just make out the island. The *island.* Suddenly, something in his mind clicked. "Well, I'll be damned," he muttered softly. "So that's what they're doing."

It was all so simple. The fishing boats that rode low in the water had no seagulls following them because their load was not fish. They carried something heavy to mask the fact that they also carried cocaine. Rettig had to be using the island as a dropping-off place for the drugs. His Canadian connections would come down and pick them up.

His adrenalin surged, sending his heart pumping at a furiously excited pace. He'd bet his seat on the board of DiFrenza's that he was right. As sure as he was about this, though, he knew what he had at the moment was only a theory. Up to this point, he hadn't been able to make any charges stick to Rettig. This time he would get absolute proof.

With one last glance at the island, he left the balcony to return to the bedroom and Caitlin. Perching on the side of the bed, he leaned over her and rained kisses over her smooth warm face.

Coming up from a cloud of sleep, she smiled softly. "It's nice being kissed awake," she murmured huskily.

"It's tolerable from my perspective too."

Her eyes slowly opened. "Good morning."

"Good morning." He kissed her, gently, lingeringly.

She blinked sleepily as he drew away. "Is it morning, by the way?"

"All the signs are pointing to it: sun, blue sky—"

She groaned and threw her arm over her eyes. "That means you're leaving."

He pulled her arm away from her face, chuckling. "I've changed my mind."

"What?" she asked, her eyes flying open. "Really?"

He nodded. "I've come up with a theory that requires my presence here. Besides, I'd feel better being here, protecting you."

He pulled back, and she pushed herself up, arranging the pillows behind her. "Why would you think I'm in danger?"

"There's a possibility that I didn't want to mention to you yesterday. Instead of trying for me and possibly failing, Rettig's men might take you hostage and use you against me. I've asked Rill to send men up to protect you. Now I'll tell him not to."

"I don't need protecting."

"Maybe you don't," he said softly, stroking her arm, "but I look at you, and everything in me wants to watch over you. And what's more, I don't see that instinct ever going away. I'm sorry."

She touched his face. "What's going on, Nico?"

"Rettig," he said succinctly. "I think I've finally figured what his men are doing here. The island."

"SwanSea's island?"

He nodded. "They're using the fishing industry of the area as a cover and the island as a drop-off and pick-up point. They fill up their specially equipped boats with something heavy to make it look as if they have a full load and are through fishing for the day. But their main cargo is cocaine. They bring it up the coast, mingling in with the regular fishing boats whenever possible. Then they drop the drugs off at the island. Sometime later, probably the next moonless night, Rettig's Canadian connections come down, load up their own boat, and take the stuff back to Canada. It's been working like a charm. They just forgot one little thing: Seagulls aren't attracted to weights. They should have thrown a few fish in, just for drill."

The idea of the island's being used for drug running was disturbing but secondary compared to her concern for Nico. She searched his face for some sign of his intentions. "So you're going to stay here and do what?"

"Don't worry, I don't plan to do anything stupid. I'm just going to keep a closer eye on the island and see if I can pick up a pattern."

"Nico—"

He touched her face. "Try to understand, Caitlin. I feel very proprietary toward Rettig. This is something I have to do. I started it, and I'm going to finish it."

"I understand what it's like to have a burning drive to succeed at something. I think all the Deverells have it; it takes a different form in each of us. But my understanding doesn't make it any easier for me to see you put your life on the line."

"Hey." He leaned over her, forming a tent of warmth and strength over her with his body. "I thought I told you, nothing's going to happen to me."

"You're not bulletproof, Nico."

He closed his eyes for a moment, trying to decide what he could possibly say that would reassure her. In the end, he decided there was nothing. "I have to do this, Caitlin, and I have to do it my way."

"I know, but that doesn't mean I have to like it."

"Causing you pain or worry hurts me more than Rettig's bullets did."

She slid her arms around his neck. "Don't spend one more minute worrying about me. Because of my love for you, my worry is bearable."

She glowed with a beauty within, he thought, and if he lived to be a hundred, he'd never deserve her. "I want to make love to you. I need to feel you against me. I need to try to make you forget, a least for a little while, that you're upset and hurting because of me."

"I need the very same thing," she whispered.

Ramona burst into the study where Caitlin was working, her face wreathed in a big smile. "Caitlin, your mother just drove up! Mr. Haines is out front helping her with her bags now."

"Great!" Jumping to her feet, she threw her pen down and turned to Nico. "Now you can meet her."

Nico had been lounging in a chair near Caitlin's desk, reading a biography of Winston Churchill. "I thought she was in Egypt."

"No, India. Now she's here."

"That's Julia," Ramona said fondly, backing out the door. "Are you two coming?"

"Of course."

She held her hand toward Nico, and he had no choice but to go with her. It wasn't that he didn't want to meet Caitlin's mother. He did. But he'd hoped to be able to put off their meeting until his problems had been settled and he was able to come down from his tightrope.

Julia Deverell was just walking in the front door as they entered the grand hall. Caitlin broke away from Nico and ran across the marble floor.

Julia threw her arms around her daughter, enveloping her in a hug and a cloud of Opium perfume. "Darling, it's so wonderful to see you. How are you?"

Caitlin drew away and gazed happily at her mother. She was as lovely as ever, her ash-brown hair falling to her shoulder in a stylishly casual fashion, her face free of any makeup, her slender figure clothed in a dark blue-silk tank top and a purple, blue, and turquoise peasant skirt. Sandals, an armful of clanky silver bracelets, and a beautiful large purple rope necklace completed the outfit. She never gave any thought to what she wore, Caitlin thought proudly, but she always looked sophisticated and elegant. "I'm terrific. How about you?"

"Couldn't be better, now that I'm back home with you. Ramona, how are you surviving the renovation?" Julia asked, bestowing a hug on the older woman.

Ramona gave a dismissive shrug. "Caitlin's doing all the work."

Julia smiled at her daughter. "I'm dying to see what you've done to the place so far."

"And I can't wait to show you. But first there's someone I want you to meet." Caitlin beckoned to Nico who had been standing to one side, watching the reunion.

But before Caitlin could perform the introduction, Mr. Haines and several of his men struggled through the door, each carrying an armload of luggage.

"Thank you, Mr. Haines. Why don't you just leave it all there." Julia gracefully waved a hand toward the door. "When I find out what bedroom Caitlin wants me in, I'll give you a call."

"Very well, Miss Deverell. And it's good to have you back."

Julia bestowed a breathtaking smile on the man. "Thank you. Caitlin, wait until you see what I brought you from India. Oh, who's this?" she asked, noticing Nico for the first time.

"This is a very special person in my life—Nico DiFrenza."

With a surprised look at her daughter's radiant face, Julia extended her hand. "It's very nice to meet you, Nico. You know, I really must stop staying away so long. I miss too much."

"Miss Deverell," he said, shaking her hand.

"Please, call me Julia. I have a feeling we're going to be getting to know each other quite well."

He grinned. "Yes, I think so. And it will be my pleasure. I can see now that Caitlin comes by her beauty quite naturally."

Humor flashed in Julia's green eyes. "I'm going to like you, aren't I?"

"Elena DiFrenza is Nico's great-grandmother," Caitlin said.

Julia lifted her brows ever so slightly. "Does that mean in the future we'll be able to get our clothes discount?"

Nico laughed. "I'm sure something can be worked out."

"Oh," Ramona said in a suddenly strange voice. "Here's Quinn, about to leave us."

Everyone turned toward the man who was standing, stone-still, in the center of the grand hall, his gaze fixed on Julia.

"*Quinn!*" Julia whispered.

Caitlin glanced at her mother and saw that all color had drained from her face. "Mother? Do you know Quinn?"

Julia, pale and motionless, stared at Quinn as if he were a ghost.

It was Quinn who finally moved. He put down his bags and walked slowly to her. "Hello, Julia," he said quietly.

"Mother? Are you all right?"

With a look at Caitlin, Quinn took Julia's arm. "Your mother and I are going into the salon and talk awhile."

Dumbfounded, Caitlin gazed after Quinn and her mother as they disappeared through a doorway. "That's the oddest thing I ever saw. They—" She broke off abruptly, because suddenly she knew . . . With an exclamation, she turned to Nico and received another shock. There was no surprise on his face.

"Quinn is my father, isn't he?"

"Yes."

"And you knew."

"Yes."

Caitlin felt as if the world had just been cut loose from its moorings and was spinning wildly through space. "I don't understand."

He took her arm, much as Quinn had taken Julia's, and tried to think of the nearest room where they could have privacy and she could sit down. "Let's go back to the study. Ramona, I wonder if we could trouble you for some tea?"

Gazing worriedly at Caitlin, Ramona nodded her head. "Of course."

On the long walk back, Caitlin was silent. Nico let her be, knowing that soon enough the numbness would wear off.

He closed the study door behind them and watched while Caitlin made her way to her desk. Instead of sitting down, she rounded on him. "What's he doing here?"

"He told me he'd just wanted to come see you."

"Me? Now?" Her laugh rang hollowly in the golden room. "Where's he been for the last twenty-six years, and why hasn't he come to see Mom in all that time?"

"You'll have to ask *him*." Her eyes widened with a pain that nearly tore him apart. "I'm sorry, Caitlin, but it's his story to tell."

"The person you had check on Quinn, he told you about him, didn't he? You knew all about this yesterday."

"The report I received gave me information on Quinn's background. When I talked with him on the bluff, he told me the rest, but he asked me not to tell you."

"*He* asked you! Nico, he's a stranger to you. You're supposed to be in love with me. You should have told me."

Nico reached out and tried to take her into his arms, but she shrugged him away. Frustrated, he ran his hand around the back of his neck. "Caitlin, Quinn didn't want to see you hurt. As a matter of fact, he told me that's why he searched my room. He saw how you felt about me and was worried about the type of man he thought I was. And of course he was absolutely right."

"What an extremely *fatherly* thing to do!"

"Caitlin—" A knock on the door interrupted. Nico opened the door and took the tea tray from Ramona.

"How are you, honey?" Ramona asked Caitlin.

"Did you know too?" she asked accusingly.

"No. But I suspected. I once saw an old photograph your mother kept in a drawer. He was a young man then, and the picture was taken from a distance." She shrugged. "I don't know. When Quinn showed up, the similarity between him and the man in the photograph struck me."

"But why did you ask him to stay?" she asked, a small cry in her voice.

Ramona clasped her hands tightly together. "I just thought it was the thing to do. I still do."

"But *why?*"

"Julia. You've said it yourself many times. She's been like a butterfly, flitting from place to place, looking for something. I personally have always believed she was looking for *someone*. Your father, I think."

Tears filled Caitlin's eyes and she sank back against the desk. "How is Mom?"

"I don't know. I'm about to take her a tray of tea too."

Caitlin nodded. "Please . . . I'd like to be alone now."

"No," Nico said. "I'm staying with you."

"Just leave."

"She'll be all right," Ramona said to him. "She needs a little time. Come with me to the kitchen, and I'll make you a cup of tea. Caitlin? You drink the tea I've brought, you hear? Nico and I will be in the kitchen if you need us."

"Caitlin?" he said, his tone pleading with her to ask him to stay.

She said nothing. And soon she was alone in the golden room she'd always thought so warm, she wrapped her arms around herself and wondered why she felt so cold.

Nine

She sought the sunshine and the sea. The heat of the sun and the power and unending rhythm of the ocean had always seemed to her a part of SwanSea and of her. She had a favorite seat—a rock that warmed in the afternoon and was lapped by waves at high tide.

It was there Quinn found her.

Somehow, he knew she would regard it an invasion of privacy if he tried to sit on the rock with her, so he stood on the sand, gazing at his daughter, his heart hurting for her, for him, for so many wasted years.

"I'd like to talk with you, Caitlin." Her gaze remained on the horizon. "Your mother's worried about you, and she wanted to come, but I asked her not to. I felt that it was my place to try and make you understand."

"Does that mean Mom understands?"

His words were cautious. This wasn't a simple situation; there would be no simple solution. "It's not something that's easily understood with just a few hours of discussion, but let me put it this way—Julia now understands more than she did."

She turned her head, and the expression in her eyes was flint hard. "Did you lie to her the way you lied to me when you told me that you had visited grandfather here?"

"You're right, Caitlin. That was a lie. It was an expedient lie, but a lie nevertheless. More than anything, I wanted the opportunity to be around you for a few days, so that I could see you and come to know you in some small way." His voice broke, and he stopped to clear his throat. "I was so hungry to know my daughter."

The charming facade he'd kept in place since he'd been here had dropped away. Now Caitlin saw signs of vulnerability that deepened the lines of his face, and she realized it was the first time she'd seen him show any real emotion. Apparently he was adept at facades. Nico had been right when he'd said Quinn had taken great care to blend into the woodwork. She looked back at the sea. "I really don't want to talk to you. Your explanations should go to Mom, not me."

"They have, and they will continue to," he said gently. "But whether you'll admit it or not, you're angry and hurt, and I don't blame you. Perhaps, though, you could simply sit there and listen to me."

Her posture was stiff, full of dignity and pain, and he felt an ache of pride and sadness in his chest as he gazed at the lovely young woman who was his daughter.

His eyes stung, and the muscles of his throat throbbed from the effort of holding back almost twenty-seven years of tears. But it wasn't the time to cry. He owed her so much, and an explanation was first and foremost. "You see, Caitlin, I met your mother twenty-seven years ago. Most of the house was closed up at that time, but Julia and her brothers had a habit of coming up from Boston from time to time to check on SwanSea and enjoy the solitude and the house where they had been raised. I was on vacation, wandering around the village, and met your mother by accident one afternoon.

"It was 1962, Caitlin, an extraordinary time. John F. Kennedy was president. Already that year John Glenn had become the first American to orbit the earth. The Peace Corps had just been established, and young people were going off to foreign countries to help those less fortunate. I felt I too could make a difference, perhaps even accomplish great things."

Caitlin had slowly turned toward him. He had at least captured her interest, he thought, however unwilling that interest was. "I was twenty-five years old with a master's degree in world economics and had a great desire to do something with my knowledge other than make money. I was eager and idealistic, and I'd agreed to take a very difficult, secret position with the government." He sighed, thinking that living the past had been a hell of a lot easier than trying to explain it. "In the fall of 1962, the Cuban missile crisis shook the world, and the following November, President Kennedy was killed. I'd been doing the work for over a year by then, and I'd lost my idealism. But by that time, it was too late. I was in something I couldn't get out of . . ."

Quinn's voice trailed off. His gaze was fixed on the horizon, but Caitlin sensed he was seeing something inside him. She waited, wanting in spite of herself to hear more about the events that had affected her mother and her father, the events that had shaped her life before she had been born.

"I loved your mother, Caitlin, you must believe that. We were together for two intense, glorious weeks. By the end of that time, I couldn't bear the thought of leaving her, but I had no choice. Everything was ready and in place for me to be slipped into a certain volatile situation. What's more, I couldn't tell her why I was leaving. One night while she slept, I left. It must have been devastating for her."

For the first time Caitlin spoke. "When I was a little girl, I used to ask where my father was. She told me my father had gone away. I asked why, and she said she had no answers, but some things weren't meant to be. She also said that she thought she must have loved you more than you loved her. I just didn't see how that was possible."

"It wasn't." Deep sorrow etched his face and aged him before her eyes. "Originally I thought I'd be back within five years. I held on to the thought that I'd see her again, and every night I'd pray that when we met again, she'd still have me. But the operation became so involved—and, by the way, so successful—I couldn't leave. I was placed in such a strategic position that if I'd pulled out, it would have meant the death of many other agents." He met her eyes. "It was a bitter pill for me. In reality, no one could really stop me from leaving, but I knew that my happiness would come at great sacrifice to others. I just couldn't do it. And there was also the very real possibility that I would be followed out of that life and into the one I truly wanted. There would have been danger for Julia, and as it turns out now, for you. Attempts to contact her could have also met with the same result. Until just recently, I didn't feel free to make inquiries. That's when I discovered I had a daughter."

She digested that. "You didn't know about me?"

"No."

"I always wondered."

"If I had known . . ." His voice trailed off, and he took a deep breath.

"Are you through with your work now?"

"Oh yes," he said most definite. "I'm really retired."

So now she knew. Finally all of her questions had been answered, but she still felt empty and flat. "Tell me, do you feel you made a difference?"

He thought for a moment. "Yes. Yes, Caitlin, I do. But I wish with all my heart I'd left it to someone else to make the difference."

The sound of the surf and the gulls couldn't disquise the fact that conversation ceased while seconds stretched to minutes.

"I have a favor to ask of you, Caitlin," he said when it became clear she wouldn't say more. "I'd like to stay here a while longer to give Julia and myself a chance to become reacquainted."

"Is that what Mom wants?"

"I hope so. I've suggested it, and I'm hoping she'll agree."

"As far as I'm concerned, it's whatever she wants."

"What about you, Caitlin? Is it too much to ask that we could get to know each other better?"

"Yes," she said after a long pause, "I think it is. You chose your path, and I grew up without a father. Now you've suddenly reappeared. Okay, fine. But I'm not affected. I see no reason why I would need a father at this point in my life."

Late that night, Nico opened the door of Caitlin's bedroom. He found her lying back against a pile of pillows, reading through a folder of correspondence.

A jade-green silk chemise stopped at the middle of her thighs, and her long legs stretched out in front of her, crossed at the ankles. She looked very relaxed, very beautiful, very unattainable.

"What are you reading?" He grimaced at his unintentionally harsh tone. He'd wanted to ask what she was doing in this room instead of his bedroom, his bed. But at the last minute, he'd decided he was afraid to hear her answer.

For some reason, Caitlin had begun to shake as soon as he'd walked in the room. As calmly as possible, she set aside the letter she'd been reading and self-consciously pulled at the hem of the chemise. "It's from an interior-decorating magazine, requesting an interview with me. They want to plan an entire issue featuring SwanSea."

"Are you going to agree?"

"Maybe." She eyed him through a thick fringe of dark lashes. Suddenly it dawned on her that it was two o'clock in the morning and he was wearing black jeans and a black sweater. "You've been out to the island, haven't you?"

"Yes."

She sat up. "Have you lost your mind? There's a full moon tonight."

"That's why I went. I figured there wouldn't be any activity out there, and I was right."

"Still, you never should have gone. How did you get out there anyway?"

"I used one of the speedboats. In case you didn't know, there're three speedboats down at the boathouse that have been refurbished to date."

She gazed at him broodingly. "I knew."

Damn. This wasn't what he wanted to talk about. "I took the smallest boat."

"And?"

"I found evidence of activity, but nothing I could use to pin on Rettig."

"So what are you going to do?"

"Keep watching. Caitlin . . ." His voice dropped and roughened. "What are you doing in here? Why aren't you in my room? Our room?"

She subsided against the pillows and linked her fingers together. "I decided I didn't want to be there tonight."

"And what about tomorrow night?" he asked, trying to be civilized. He wanted to jerk her into his arms and make love to her until she had no energy left to be upset with him. "Where do you think you'll want to be then?"

"I don't know."

He sat down beside her on the bed. She started to scramble off the other side, but he caught her wrist, keeping her where she was. "Caitlin, I know you're hurt and confused, but please don't stay away from me. Let's work it out together."

She should have been quicker; she should never have let him get this close. His presence had a way of endangering her equilibrium. She tried to jerk away, but he held her tight.

"I'm not confused, Nico. As a matter of fact, it all seems crystal clear to me. I feel your first consideration should have been to me, not honoring some pledge to Quinn that you wouldn't tell me." Tears formed in her eyes, making them glisten like jewels.

"You were my first consideration, honey. I was trying to protect you."

"I don't need protecting, dammit! I've told you time and time again."

"Oh, right. You're a Deverell. You're tough. Well, big deal, Caitlin. I'm not impressed."

"I don't care."

"Well, I do, and it just seemed to me that having a father appear out of the blue like that wasn't something that should be sprung on you."

"You mean like it was?"

"Exactly. And as I told you, it was Quinn's story to tell."

She gazed down at her hands. "You think I'm being unreasonable, don't you?"

"No, not at all. You've received a tremendous shock. I just don't think you've let yourself feel that shock yet."

"Then let me, Nico. Just back off and let me."

He stared at her for a long minute, then sighed. "I can't. I wish I could do as you ask, but I can't. I have this great urge to cushion all your shocks and blows for you."

"You just don't listen to me, do you?" she cried.

"I always listen to you, but I admitted to you days ago that I'm a bastard. Remember I also said in spite of all my sins and crimes, I love you. And because I do, I'm enough of a bastard to stay here in your room if you won't come back to mine." He took her arms and twisted her around and down until she lay on the bed.

She struggled against him. "Nico, I don't want to do this. Let's talk—"

"No. If we talk, you'll have a chance to argue with me, and an argument will only drive another wedge between us. I'm not willing to take that chance. You mean too much to me."

He pressed his mouth to hers, intending to do no more than gently brush his lips against hers, comfort her, let her know how much he loved her. But he quickly realized that wasn't what either of them wanted. He could feel the tension changing in her as she grew softer, more pliable, and it made him want to join with her in love and fire and know the feeling of coming apart in her arms.

Impatiently, he stripped off her panties and entered her.

But once sheathed to the hilt in her, he stilled and met her eyes. "Tell me you want me." His words were a demand, but his tone was begging.

She arched up to him and grasped his buttocks with her hands, trying to pull him deeper. "I want you. Lord, how I want you."

He began to move inside her, hard and fast, bringing to her and to him a burning, a wildness, a great love.

Dark clouds boiled on the horizon; razor-edged white lightning streaked out of the heavens and bolted straight down to the water. The wind had picked up and blew cool against Caitlin's face. She could see the storm far out at sea and knew it would be sweeping in over the land soon. She'd go in then, but not until.

Sitting on the thick green carpet of grass, she clasped her hands around her knees and lifted her face to the wind, inhaling the energy and the freshness of air that had never before touched land. There was an exhilaration to a storm at SwanSea that she'd never felt anywhere else.

She heard a jangle of silver, caught a whiff of Opium, and her mother dropped to the grass beside her. "I love watching storms," she murmured, without looking around.

"I know," Julia said ruefully. "I can remember more than once trying to find you during a storm, only to discover you standing out here, the wind and the rain whipping around you. You were such a fierce little thing. I always had the feeling you felt that you and SwanSea together could weather anything."

Caitlin couldn't help but smile, because she had felt exactly that way. "I've grown up. I'm older and wiser now."

"But yet I still find you out here."

"The storm isn't here yet." She turned to her mother. With her smooth, unlined skin and wind-tossed hair, Julia still looked as lovely as a young girl, Caitlin thought. "How *are* you, Mom? We really haven't had a chance to talk."

"I think I'm gradually getting over the shock. How about you?"

"The same. I've caught glimpses of you and Quinn over the last two days. How are things going?"

Julia shrugged. "I don't know. I'm enjoying this time with him, but . . ."

"But?"

"It's too soon to tell. We've been apart for a great many years. And when you think about it, we were really together only two weeks."

"Ramona told me she's always felt you were searching for someone, that that's why you've traveled so much."

"If I have, it hasn't been conscious." Her lips pursed thoughtfully. "Do you know that Quinn and I have discovered we were often in the same country at the same time? A lot of times even in the same city. If we'd turned a particular corner at a particular moment, we might have seen each other. It's ironic."

"I think it's sad," Caitlin said.

"That too. At any rate, whatever happens, I'm glad I finally know why he left me."

"You thought he'd left you because he didn't love you enough to stay. You had to have been bitter about that, but if you were, you did a beautiful job of keeping it from me."

"Oh, I was definitely bitter for a while." She laughed shortly. "I am human, darling. But then you came along, and I knew that no matter what, I'd thank Quinn my whole life long for you."

Tears welled into Caitlin's eyes. "I really love you, Mom, and I admire you so much."

Julia made a short, dismissing sound. "You put me in the shade, my darling daughter. I would never even have considered attempting what you are doing here with SwanSea." She reached out and stroked Caitlin's hair. "Quinn told me that you have the same color hair his mother had. I always wondered where that gorgeous cinnamon shade came from." She smiled gently and searched for some sign of what Caitlin was feeling. "I'm worried about you. I want you to know that I understand your hesitancy about Quinn. After all, you must have felt terribly abandoned all these years."

The odd need to comfort her mother wasn't new, she realized. She'd known the urge when she was growing up, and now she knew why. "I had you and the family and just about all the love any one person could handle."

Julia sighed, knowing Caitlin wasn't ready to address the issue of her father. "I won't press you, darling, but I hope that in the future you'll find a way to make peace with Quinn. He needs you, and I think if you'll let yourself, you'll come to realize that you need him. But . . . Nico . . ."

Caitlin groaned. "Mother."

"Yes, I know. You'd like me to stay out of it, and I'm going to. I just want to say that over the last couple of days, I've really grown to like him, and it's obvious to me that he loves and cares about you a great deal. Don't hold it against him because he didn't tell you about Quinn. I think it's completely natural and honorable that he should feel Quinn or I should be the one to break such enormous news to you."

"I know," she murmured. The storm was closer now. Caitlin could smell the salt and sulfurous scent in the wind and could feel the electric charge on her skin. The storm would be violent and short. "I know," she said again.

By midnight, the storm had blown over. She and SwanSea had survived another storm, Caitlin reflected. Usually the thought exhilarated her, but tonight, as she wandered restlessly around Nico's bedroom waiting for him, she felt strangely flat. The melodic refrain of "Someone to Watch Over Me" was playing on her tape recorder. It reminded her of the night she had stood wrapped in enchantment and Nico's arms while the song had flowed around them, and the memory made her feel even more restless.

Disturbed, she opened the bedroom's French windows and gazed up at the overcast sky. Every once in a while, the moon would break free of the clouds and shine with a silver luminosity. But its freedom lasted mere moments, and then new clouds formed a shroud.

The words of the song drifted through the haze of her thoughts: ". . . someone to watch over me."

To try to shield someone you love from being hurt was a part of loving. Nico tried to watch over her; she worried about him. This man Rettig had nearly killed him, and now it appeared Rettig was close again.

Suddenly, her gaze flew back to the overcast sky.

"Oh, my Lord," she whispered. "Nico's gone out to the island."

She left the room, her single thought to help Nico. It was only the sight of Quinn quietly leaving her mother's room that stopped her cold.

When Quinn glanced around and saw her, his first reaction was guilt that Caitlin had seen him coming from Julia's room so late at night. He quickly banished the feeling. "I'm sorry if this upsets you, Caitlin, but your mother and I owe you no explanation."

"You're right," she said quietly. "Excuse me."

She started past him, but he caught her arm. "Wait a minute. There's something wrong. I can tell it by your face. What is it? Where are you going?"

She pulled against his hold, but surprisingly his grip tightened. "Quinn, I don't have time for this. Let me go."

"I may be retired, Caitlin, but all my agent instincts are still in place. What is it? Is Nico in trouble?"

She made a sound halfway between anger and a sob. "Yes. He's gone out to the island."

Quinn's eyes narrowed. "The island. Of course. I thought there was something strange . . . What is it? Drugs?"

She nodded, almost frantic. "Now will you let me go?"

"Yes, but I'm coming with you."

"No—"

"I'm coming with you, Caitlin, but first we need to stop by my room."

A short time later, the two of them were in a speedboat, plowing through the dark waves toward the island—Quinn at the wheel, Caitlin beside him.

Before this, she reflected, she'd seen only the pleasant, charming side of him. The past twenty minutes had shown her the steel that had apparently made him so important to the government.

The sea was wild tonight. Spray dampened her skin, blackness enveloped them. She knew these waters well, but she had to admit that she was glad Quinn was with her.

"It shouldn't be too much farther," she called.

He shut off the engines. "We'll paddle in from here. We don't want to alert anyone we're coming."

She nodded and said a fervent prayer that Nico was all right.

Ten

The flashlights on the table cast broad beams of light on the two men standing in the center of the pitch-black room. Crouched behind the dustcovered couch, Nico listened, unable to believe his good luck. Not only was Rettig here but also Rettig's main Canadian contact, Marcus Kozera. The two men had never been seen together.

"This island couldn't be better," Kozera was saying. "We've made two successful runs, but tonight is our biggest shipment yet, and I wanted to be here to check it out for myself. It's good."

"I told you so," Rettig said with satisfaction. "It's never used, isolated from normal shipping routes, and hell, it even has this house on it." He laughed.

"What about DiFrenza? I'm going to sleep a lot better at night when he's finally dead and buried."

"There've been too many people around that house for a regular hit. This time, I want it to look like an accident, so there aren't a bunch of cops swarming around afterward. He's running longer distances now. Within the next few days, he should have an established route. It'll be easy to take him out then."

"Good."

Rettig laughed. "Right before I kill him I'm going to thank him for leading us to this island."

Behind the couch, Nico tensed, his hand tightening on his gun.

A man's voice burst suddenly into the room, tinny and loud, through a walkie-talkie. "Rettig?"

"Yeah?"

"We've got a woman and a man here. Seems they were trying to crash the party."

"Who are they?"

"Never saw them before in my life, but I'd sure like to get to know *her.*"

A cold sweat broke out over Nico. Caitlin and Quinn—it had to be. Dammit. All this situation needed was another complication. He was going to have to rearrange his plans fast. Nothing could happen to Caitlin . . .

"Bring them here," Rettig said. "Kozera, you know anything about this?"

"No, but I don't like it."

"Don't worry about it. We'll take care of them. Besides, the risk is why we make so damn much money."

Before Kozera could answer, the door opened.

"Don't hurt her," Nico heard Quinn say. Nico brought his gun up into firing position. Carefully, he peered over the couch. He could just make out the forms of Caitlin and Quinn. The darkness and Rettig and Kozera's movements made it risky for him to get off a shot—and the terrifying chance that he might hit Caitlin kept him still.

"I'm fine," Caitlin said, trying to reassure Quinn. The last time she'd gotten a good look at him, there'd been blood trickling down the side of his face. The man who had come up behind them had struck Quinn for trying to protect her.

"Where'd you find them, Larry?" Rettig asked.

"Josh radioed me from the boat that he'd spotted these two heading toward the beach on the east side of the island. I made it a point to be there when they beached."

"Good job. So . . . who are *you*?"

Be careful what you say, Nico silently coaxed Caitlin. He wasn't sure if revealing she was a Deverell would make matters worse or not, but it would be fatal if she asked what they'd done with him.

It was Quinn who answered Rettig. "I'm Quinn O'Neill, and this is my daughter, Caitlin. Our boat conked out on us, and we were trying to find some shelter until morning."

"They're lying," Kozera said.

"Use your head," Rettig snapped with irritation. "Why would they walk into a situation like this?"

"He had a gun," Larry said.

Rettig's tone turned ominous. "Really?"

"Sharks," Caitlin said quickly and managed a shudder. "I've seen all the *Jaws* movies. I wanted to be prepared. Look, if you'll just let us go, we'll—"

Kozera laughed. "You'll what? Paddle your way back to wherever you came from and use the first phone you find to call the police? I don't think so."

"You talk too much, Kozera," Rettig said coldly. "It doesn't matter where they came from or where they think they're going." He drew his gun. "Larry, get back out there and guard the shipment. We won't be much longer. We'll take care of these two, and then we'll join you."

Larry left the cottage. Behind the couch, Nico prepared to make his move.

Caitlin could feel herself trembling, but there was too much to think about to be sidetracked by fear. Desperately she tried to rule out all emotion that could block clear thinking. She would never know where Nico was unless they could get out of here alive. She thought her knowledge of the island would give her and Quinn the advantage, but first they had to get away. "Maybe we could make a deal," she began.

Rettig's teeth flashed in the darkness. "I'd love to, sweetheart, but unfortunately I have pressing business. And business always come first." He cocked his gun.

"No!" With blind instinct she started toward the gun.

"Get out of here, Caitlin!" Quinn yelled as he shoved her out of the way and hurled himself past her at the two men.

As Caitlin lost her balance and crashed to the floor, Rettig's gun went off, and Nico vaulted the sofa and launched himself toward Kozera and Rettig. He swung the butt of his gun against Rettig's temple and followed up with a karate chop to Kozera's neck.

In less than a minute, it was over, and Nico was reaching for Caitlin. "My God, are you all right?"

"Yes." Her elbow ached, having caught most of her weight when she had fallen, but it didn't seem important. "I'm so glad you're here. I was so afraid for you. Oh heavens, what about Quinn?"

"Quinn?" Nico asked, cradling Caitlin against his chest.

"He got me, but it's just a flesh wound." His voice was calm and steady.

"You're shot?" Caitlin said, struggling to see, but Quinn was lying in the shadows.

"Stay where you are," he said. "I'll be all right. You were wonderful, by the way."

"Not as wonderful as you," she said, meaning it with all her heart.

"Nico, sorry you had to take those two out by yourself."

Nico stroked Caitlin's hair, wishing he could see her more clearly. He'd known a terrible rage when Rettig had pointed his gun at her. "No problem."

"So I noticed," Quinn said, his tone dry.

Nico could tell that Quinn was making a terrible effort to keep his words even. The man was in trouble, he thought, and he'd bet money it was more than a flesh wound. "Save your strength. Don't try to move. We'll get you out of here as fast as we can."

The door opened, and a flashlight beam panned around the room. "Nico?" a deep voice called.

"About time you got here," Nico said sharply.

Footsteps crossed the floor toward them. "Give me a break. There were two boats out there, you know, with two men on each of them. That makes *four* in case you've forgotten how to add. Of course, I did have an advantage, being from Texas and all."

The flashlight swept the floor, finding Quinn, then the two men who lay incapacitated on the floor. When the light reached Nico and Caitlin, it bypassed Nico and went straight to Caitlin. She dropped her eyes from the glare of the light and saw the pointed toes of a pair of snakeskin cowboy boots.

"Is this Caitlin?" the deep voice asked.

"Yes, and get that damned light off us."

The light stayed perfectly steady. "Glad to meet you, ma'am. Amarillo Smith at your service."

The blades of the helicopter sliced powerfully through the air, making a loud rushing sound as it squatted on the beach, waiting for its passengers. Holding Quinn's hand, Caitlin bent over his stretcher. "We've contacted Julia. She'll meet you at the hospital."

"That's very kind of you." He tried to pat her hand

and grimaced with pain. "You're not to worry about me. It's nothing, you know."

"I know." She was surprised to find her eyes filling with tears. On the other side of him, Nico applied a pressure bandage to the wound in Quinn's chest. "Quinn, when the hospital lets you go, I want you to come back to SwanSea to recuperate. Ramona and I can look after you. I'm sure Mom will be there too. SwanSea can be a little hectic with all the work that's going on, but Nico was able to regain his strength there, and so will you."

"Are you sure, Caitlin?" Quinn asked.

She wiped at her eyes and smiled down at him. "I'm sure." A quick glance told her that the medics were ready to put him aboard the helicopter. She pressed a kiss to his forehead. "I'll see you soon."

The helicopter lifted off into the approaching dawn. Nico took a firm grip on her arms and turned her to face him. "It was very brave of you to come out here after me, Caitlin, and maybe I'll appreciate it after I get over remembering how damned scared I was when I saw the danger you'd walked into. But if you *ever* do anything that stupid again, I will strangle you."

He kissed her with a ferocity that showed her how much he loved her. When he broke off the kiss, it was a moment before their breathing returned to normal.

"Let's go home," he said. "Rill can clean things up here. There's something there I have to show you."

In front of one of the attic windows, Caitlin chose a spot that was just beginning to warm with the sun and sank to the floor. Not too far away, Nico lifted the lid of a trunk and rummaged through it.

Caitlin watched him curiously as he lifted a loosely wrapped package from the trunk, walked to her, and dropped down beside her. "Here it is—Elena's bible. Inside you'll find her letter of explanation, along with her marriage certificate."

"Then it's all true."

"I'm afraid there's no doubt."

"Afraid? Why?"

"Caitlin, I want to assure you that the DiFrenzas want nothing from the Deverells. I know that's hard for you to believe, and your family will probably find it impossible to believe. Very few people have as much money as the Deverells, but we have more than we'll ever need in our lifetime, with enough left over for the generations to come.

"Remember that first night when I said I wouldn't be able to afford to stay here? I said that out of habit. Ever since I graduated from law school, I've made it a point to live on my salary. But that doesn't mean I don't have enough money to give you everything you'll ever want." She made a dismissive motion with her hand, but he hurried on. "And it's not the Deverell name either. My family has proudly carried the name of DiFrenza for generations. We will continue to do so."

"Nico—"

Unconsciously, he shifted closer to her, anxious to make her understand. "But it's Elena, don't you see? Stubbornly, she's held on to her secret all these years. But now she's ill, and she wanted us to know what happened. I promised her I would try to find this package, and for her sake, I'm glad I did. It's evidence that she and a young man named John Deverell once loved and dreamed of a future together. Now she can live out what time remains of her life in peace.

"But this changes nothing for you and me. As a lawyer, I can tell you that your inheritance is absolutely safe, but if it will make you feel any better, I'll sign a prenuptial agreement giving up all claim to SwanSea and your money."

She felt an aching lump of tenderness grow in her throat. "Aren't you overlooking something? Forget the money. You're a *Deverell*, Nico. You're part of SwanSea. You're Edward's great-great-grandson."

"I haven't overlooked that, but it won't affect us. We're second or third half cousins, once removed—or something like that."

"That's not what I mean. I think we're missing something very significant here. My grandfather once told me that Edward's two burning obsessions were SwanSea and having a large family. Who knows what really happened back then, but whatever did, our side of the family never knew about you, and your side of the family never knew about us. But now, through our marriage and our children, we will restore the line that was broken so long ago."

"Does that mean? . . ."

"Nico, a few hours ago, I was staring into the barrel of a loaded gun, and I didn't know if you were dead or alive. Compared to that, everything else pales. Except the love I have for you." She laughed. "My grandfather would get the biggest kick out of this. And I think this news is wonderful. I can't wait to tell the rest of the family."

Relief flowed through his body with a force that had him trembling, and he didn't even notice that his face was damp from tears of joy. "Thank God," he said softly. "Thank God."

For the moment, the idea of Edward, his dreams, and his house weren't real or important to him. Maybe someday they would be, but for now, only the woman before him had meaning and importance. "Will you marry me, Caitlin?"

"Yes, my darling, I'll marry you. Here at SwanSea,

with both our families around us. We'll hire an entire army of doctors, nurses, planes, ambulances—whatever it takes—but I want our very special guest to be Elena."

"That would be absolutely right and perfect," he whispered.

For a moment, he allowed himself to bask in the warmth and love of Caitlin's eyes. There had been times in the last few terrifying hours when he'd thought he would lose her. But there she was, warm and generous, giving and loving. He leaned forward and kissed her gently. There had been enough words. He wanted to show her how much he loved her, how all the days of his life, he would cherish and adore her.

Caitlin slipped her tongue between his lips, deepening the kiss and lying back on the sun-heated floor, pulling him with her. She felt swamped by a tidal wave of love and happiness. Her world had once consisted of her family and SwanSea. Now Nico was in her world, filling it to bursting.

Perhaps they'd been luckier than the Deverells and the DiFrenzas that had gone before them. Somehow, they'd been able to hold their dream. They had survived the events of last night, and now another day was beginning. Soon the workmen would arrive, and later she would visit her father. But for now, she and Nico badly needed the passion and fire that only the could give each other.

The morning sun continued to rise, its streams of light surrounding the two lovers with warmth. And outside, in the sun's golden rays, the windows shone, as if the great house SwanSea were smiling.

THE EDITOR'S CORNER

We suspect that Cupid comes to visit our Bantam offices every year when we're preparing the Valentine's Day books. It seems we're always specially inspired by the one exclusively romantic holiday in the year. And our covers next month reflect just how inspired we were . . . by our authors who also must have had a visit from the chubby cherub. They shimmer with cherry-red metallic ink and are presents in and of themselves—as are the stories within. They range from naughty to very nice!

First, we bring you Suzanne Forster's marvelous **WILD CHILD**, LOVESWEPT #384. Cat D'Angelo had been the town's bad girl and Blake Wheeler its golden boy when the young assistant D.A. had sent her to the reformatory for suspected car theft. Now, ten years later, she has returned to work as a counselor to troubled kids—and to even the score with the man who had hurt her so deeply! Time had only strengthened the powerful forces that drew them together . . . and Blake felt inescapable hunger for the beautiful, complicated hellcat who could drive a man to ruin—or to ecstasy. Could the love and hate Cat had held so long in her heart be fused by the fire of mutual need and finally healed by passion? We think you'll find **WILD CHILD** delicious—yet calorie free—as chocolates packaged in a red satin box!

Treat yourself to a big bouquet with Gail Douglas's *The Dreamweavers:* **BEWITCHING LADY**, LOVESWEPT #385. When the Brawny Josh Campbell who looked as if he could wield a sword as powerfully as any clansman stopped on a deserted road to give her a ride, Heather Sinclair played a mischievous Scottish lass to the hilt, beguiling the moody but fascinating man whose gaze hid inner demons . . . and hinted at a dangerous passion she'd never known. Josh felt his depression lift after months of despair, but he was too cynical to succumb to this delectable minx's appeal . . . or was he? A true delight!

Sweet, fresh-baked goodies galore are yours in Joan
(continued)

Elliott Pickart's **MIXED SIGNALS,** LOVESWEPT #386. Katha Logan threw herself into Vince Santini's arms, determined to rescue the rugged ex-cop from the throng of reporters outside city hall. Vince enjoyed being kidnapped by this lovely and enchanting nut who drove like a madwoman and intrigued him with her story of a crime he just *had* to investigate . . . with her as his partner! Vince believed that a man who risked his life for a living had no business falling in love. Katha knew she could cherish Vince forever if he'd let her, but playing lovers' games wasn't enough anymore. Could they learn to fly with the angels and together let their passions soar?

We give a warm, warm greeting—covered with hearts, with flowers—to a new LOVESWEPT author, but one who's not new to any of us who treasure romances. Welcome Lori Copeland, who brings us LOVESWEPT #387, **DARLING DECEIVER,** next month. Bestselling mystery writer Shae Malone returned to the sleepy town where he'd spent much of his childhood to finish his new novel, but instead of peace and quiet, he found his home invaded by a menagerie of zoo animals temporarily living next door . . . with gorgeously grown-up Harriet Whitlock! As a teenager she'd chased him relentlessly, embarrassed him with poems declaring everlasting love, but now she was an exquisite woman whose long-legged body made him burn with white-hot fire. Harri still wanted Shae with shameless abandon, but did she dare risk giving her heart again?

Your temperature may rise when you read **HEART-THROB** by Doris Parmett, LOVESWEPT #388. Hannah Morgan was bright, eager, beautiful—an enigma who filled television director Zack Matthews with impatience . . . and a sizzling hunger. The reporter in him wanted to uncover her mysteries, while the man simply wanted to gaze at her in moonlight. Hannah was prepared to work as hard as she needed to satisfy the workaholic heartbreaker . . . until her impossibly virile boss crumbled her defenses with tenderness and ignited a hunger she'd never expected to feel again. Was she
(continued)

willing to fight to keep her man? Don't miss this sparkling jewel of a love story. A true Valentine's Day present.

For a great finish to a special month, don't miss Judy Gill's **STARGAZER**, LOVESWEPT #389, a romance that shines with the message of the power of love . . . at any age. As the helicopter hovered above her, Kathy M'Gonigle gazed with wonder at her heroic rescuer, but stormy-eyed Gabe Fowler was furious at how close she'd come to drowning in the sudden flood—and shocked at the joy he felt at touching her again! Years before, he'd made her burn with desire, but she'd been too young and he too restless to settle down. Now destiny had brought them both home. Could the man who put the stars in her eyes conquer the past and promise her forever?

All our books—well, their authors wish they could promise you forever. That's not possible, but authors and staff can wish you wonderful romance reading.

Now it is my great pleasure to give you one more Valentine's gift—namely, to reintroduce you to our Susann Brailey, now Senior Editor, who will grace these pages in the future with her fresh and enthusiastic words. But don't think for a minute that you're getting rid of me! I'll be here—along with the rest of the staff—doing the very best to bring you wonderful love stories all year long.

As I have told you many times in the past, I wish you peace, joy, and the best of all things—the love of family and friends.

Carolyn Nichols

Carolyn Nichols
Editor
LOVESWEPT
Bantam Books
666 Fifth Avenue
New York, NY 10103

FAN OF THE MONTH

Joni Clayton

It's really great fun to be a LOVESWEPT Fan of the Month as it provides me with the opportunity to publicly thank Carolyn Nichols, Bantam Books, and some of my favorite authors: Sandra Brown, Iris Johansen, Kay Hooper, Fayrene Preston, Helen Mittermeyer and Deborah Smith (to name only a few!).

My good friend, Mary, first introduced me to romance fiction and LOVESWEPTS in 1984 as an escape from the pressures of my job. Almost immediately my associates noticed the difference in my disposition and attitude and questioned the reason for the change. They all wanted to thank LOVESWEPT!

It did not take me long to discover that most romance series were inconsistent in quality and were not always to my liking—but not LOVESWEPT. I have thoroughly enjoyed each and every volume. All were "keepers" . . . so of course I wanted to own the entire series. I enlisted the aid of friends and used book dealers. Presto! The series was complete! As soon as LOVESWEPT was offered through the mail, I subscribed and have never missed a copy!

I have since retired from the "hurly-burly" of the working world and finally have the time to start to reread all of my LOVESWEPT "keepers."

To Carolyn, all of the authors, and the LOVESWEPT staff—Thanks for making my retirement so enjoyable!

60 Minutes to a Better, More Beautiful You!

Now it's easier than ever to awaken your sensuality, stay slim forever—even make yourself irresistible. With Bantam's bestselling subliminal audio tapes, you're only 60 minutes away from a better, more beautiful you!

__ 45004-2	**Slim Forever**	$8.95
__ 45112-X	**Awaken Your Sensuality**	$7.95
__ 45081-6	**You're Irresistible**	$7.95
__ 45035-2	**Stop Smoking Forever**	$8.95
__ 45130-8	**Develop Your Intuition**	$7.95
__ 45022-0	**Positively Change Your Life**	$8.95
__ 45154-5	**Get What You Want**	$7.95
__ 45041-7	**Stress Free Forever**	$7.95
__ 45106-5	**Get a Good Night's Sleep**	$7.95
__ 45094-8	**Improve Your Concentration**	$7.95
__ 45172-3	**Develop A Perfect Memory**	$8.95

THE DELANEY DYNASTY

Men and women whose loves an passions are so glorious it takes many great romance novels by three bestselling authors to tell their tempestuous stories.

THE SHAMROCK TRINITY

THE DELANEYS OF KILLAROO

THE DELANEYS: *The Untamed Years*